The Witchfinder's Familiar

Spoiler Warning

The stories in this anthology contain spoilers from the first two books in The Witches of Windsor series.

Other books by Rande Goodwin

The Witches of Windsor

The Witchfinder's Serpent

The Witchfinder's Sacrifice

The Witches of Windsor

The Witchfinder's Familiar

RANDE GOODWIN

With a story by
Joseph J. Christiano

Published by Lonely Mountain Press

Design and composition by Rande Goodwin
Images obtained from and/or used under license from Freepik.com

ISBN: 979-8-9925536-0-4 (Hardcover)
ISBN: 979-8-218-42177-9 (Hardcover, special full color edition)
ISBN: 979-8-218-42178-6 (eBook)

Printed on acid-free paper

First Edition

www.randegoodwin.com

Contents

JENN: PART I

Jenn Quigley pumped the pedals of her red bicycle down Windsor Avenue, the breeze tossing her curly brown hair. It was a beautiful sunny day, school was out, and for the first time in nearly a month, she felt unburdened by the events that had been plaguing the town. Up ahead on the right was her destination: the Watson mansion, the massive three-story Victorian home of her friend Nate and his family.

Three weeks ago, she had helped Nate banish the evil warlock, Malleus Hodge, at the battle of the Old Burying Ground. It had been the turning point in a war of lies, madness, and fear that Hodge had set in motion, a modern-day witch hysteria that had plunged the town into chaos. In the process, Jenn had learned that magick was real and that she herself was a witch. Unfortunately, she knew little on the topic of witchcraft. Fortunately, however, she knew someone who did. Nate's Aunt Celia was a powerful and experienced witch and with any luck, before the day was through, Jenn would learn a thing or two about it herself.

As Jenn neared the Watson mansion, she yanked the bike's handlebars, jumping the bike over the curb and onto the sidewalk. She slowed slightly as she approached a gap in the hedge that bordered the property. Passing through it, she glided the bike up the stone walkway until she came to a stop at the mansion's front porch.

Jenn looked at the building in front of her. Nate's house was a marvel of nineteenth-century architecture. The porch itself was immense. It wrapped around the tall brick structure, its huge white pillars stretching skyward to support the overhanging roof. From where she stood, Jenn knew, there was a lot she *couldn't* see, from the second floor's stained-glass windows to the widow's walk at the mansion's pinnacle. On previous visits, she had toured the house, inside and out, and it continued to amaze her.

Jenn hopped off the bike, set the kickstand, and hurried up the wide wooden steps to the front door. As she reached for the doorbell, the heavy door swung silently inward, and a familiar face appeared.

"Hey, Jenn!" It was Nate, and he was smiling. "Aunt Celia said you were coming. I saw you through the window. Come on in!"

Jenn was happy to see him. "Hi, Nate," she replied, her smile matching his. After a quick hug, she followed him through the door and into the foyer. Intricate woodwork and old-fashioned wallpaper decorated the walls from floor to ceiling. Doorways branched off in several directions. The grand staircase stretched upward to the right, curving back on itself as it approached the second floor.

"Listen," said Nate, turning to her. "Marc's helping me with something in the basement. It's for tomorrow's Art Expo at the public library. Aunt Celia's in the artifact room, if you want to head on up. She said you offered to help her with something?"

"Yeah, that's right," said Jenn. *And hopefully she can help me as well,* she thought. "I'll see you in a bit?"

"Absolutely," said Nate. With a nod, he turned and hurried through one of the doorways toward another part of the house.

Jenn moved swiftly up the stairs to the second floor. She'd been there frequently enough to know the way. The artifact room was Aunt Celia's workshop. It had once been off limits to Nate and his brother, Marc. More recently, however, they'd been using it as a conference room of sorts. After passing several unused bedrooms, each one guest-ready and decorated in antique period furniture, Jenn found the one doorway she sought. She walked through to find Aunt Celia seated at the artifact room's center table, paging through an old book. Shelves and display cases full of crystals and objects, mysterious and arcane, lined three of the walls. A fireplace with its intricate, towering mantelpiece decorated the fourth. Aunt Celia looked up as Jenn approached.

"Jenn," said Aunt Celia, sliding out of her chair and standing. She adjusted her hair, which was bound in a tidy blonde bun. "Thank you for coming! I'm excited to have your help."

"No problem," Jenn replied with a smile. "I'm happy to do it." She pushed her glasses up the bridge of her nose with a finger. "Is that it?" Jenn pointed to an old backpack sitting on the table, its top flap torn open.

"Yes," said Aunt Celia. "Shall we get started?"

"Sure—may I?" Jenn reached for the pack and, at Aunt Celia's nod, pulled it toward herself. Spreading the ripped fabric, she reached inside and gently pulled out one of several stacks of old paper. She then removed others, setting each one down on the table in front of her. The yellowed pages were covered in Latin script penned in a mixture of inks, some dark, some faded, all of them very old. Small images and symbols appeared randomly throughout. Some of the pages had scorch marks while others appeared water damaged.

Finally, after removing everything else, Jenn retrieved the remains of an old leather binding from the very bottom of the pack. Its front and back covers were weathered and cracked. She placed it on the table beside the piles of paper.

Jenn recognized the ruined pieces of the old grimoire. It was from this book, once owned by her own grandmother, that they'd obtained the spell to banish Malleus Hodge. It had been damaged during the battle, its pages scattered on the wind. Marc had gathered what he could find that day in the cemetery. He'd placed the collected sheets in the torn backpack he'd brought with him. And now, she and Aunt Celia were going to try to reassemble its pieces.

A sickly stench reached Jenn's nostrils. It was coming from the old grimoire. "Did it smell like this before?" she asked Aunt Celia with a grimace. Jenn didn't think so.

Aunt Celia shrugged, wrinkling her nose. "Not that I remember." She walked over to a large window and lifted the sash. "Some fresh air might help though. It *is* a very old book."

Jenn nodded as her eyes studied the table. "So where do we begin? The pages aren't numbered, and sadly, my Latin isn't strong."

"Yes," replied Aunt Celia. "It'll be a challenge. Perhaps we should treat it like a jigsaw puzzle, you know? Try matching the pages by their appearance. The spells were scribed at different times with different inks. We may be able to determine which ones go together that way."

"That's a good idea," said Jenn. She began sifting through the stacks of paper.

"When we're done, I have a spell that will reattach the individual sheets to the binding, a magickal superglue, so to speak." Aunt Celia smiled. "Oh," she said, her face suddenly serious. "Remember—don't speak any of the words you see out loud. The spells in this book are dangerous and we wouldn't want any . . . incidents."

"Got it." Jenn nodded, returning to her page shuffling. She remembered the warnings Aunt Celia and Tee, another powerful witch and Aunt Celia's friend, had given her when they'd prepared Hodge's banishing spell. They'd stressed how important it was to follow the instructions to the letter. Words, pronunciation, spell components—everything had to be perfect. If any part of it went astray, well, the results could be disastrous.

In the end, Jenn had performed the spell on her own—and it had worked. The memory was still fresh in her mind—sitting in the church, the spell components in front of her as she spoke the spell's incantation from memory. She remembered the decaying human hand, the grisliest of the spell's components, lying at the center of the circle, the other components piled on top. Whose hand was it, and where had it come from? She hadn't had the courage to ask and wasn't sure she wanted the answer. At the moment, in any event, so many other questions took precedence.

"Listen." Jenn paused, looking at Aunt Celia. "While I'm here, I was hoping to talk to you about something. Several things, actually. I wanted to ask you—I mean, I don't know anything about—" Her voice dropped off. She wasn't sure how to broach the topic.

"You wanted to ask me about magick? About being a witch?" said Aunt Celia with a knowing smile.

"Yes! Exactly!" A sense of relief filled Jenn. "I know *nothing*—and I want to know *everything*!"

"I figured as much." Aunt Celia chuckled. "It was one of the reasons I invited you over. I was in your situation once, and it was your ancestor, Lydia Gilbert, who taught me everything I desperately needed to know. Ask me anything."

Jenn looked around the room excitedly. A flood of questions filled her head. "I want to know more about spells and spell components. Will I get an innate ability like yours? What about an animal familiar—" She frowned, cocking her head. "I don't think I want one, is that a requirement?"

Aunt Celia laughed. "Slow down. Let's take one thing at a time." She motioned to an empty chair before pulling one out for herself. Aunt Celia sat and Jenn followed suit. "Let's talk first about innate abilities—as you know I can communicate with animals and other small creatures." She gestured toward the open window where a swarm of butterflies appeared. Jenn watched in amazement as they fluttered about, slowly circling the table in a single cloud. "Did you know that a group of butterflies is called a kaleidoscope?"

"That's so cool!" Jenn exclaimed. The butterflies made a second lap around the table before disappearing back through the window, fluttering off into the summer sky.

"But how or when will I know if I have an ability like that?" Jenn asked.

"Well, my magick surfaced after I came in contact with my mother's familiar for the first time. Sometimes one form of magick can draw out another.

There's no way to know for sure what your innate ability will be or when it will appear, but believe me—you'll know when it happens."

At that moment, Jenn heard a flapping of wings at the window. Corvin the crow, Aunt Celia's familiar, appeared on the sill.

"Hello, Mr.—uh, I mean Corvin," said Jenn. The crow hopped into the air and glided to the table, his wings ruffling the pages that lay scattered about.

"And I couldn't live without my familiar of course," continued Aunt Celia. She smiled fondly at the bird. The crow let out a squawk. "Corvin has helped me in more ways than I can ever describe. He's been my companion for literally centuries, and I'm grateful for every moment we've been together."

Corvin warbled softly for a moment, and Jenn could tell that he and Aunt Celia were communicating.

"Yes, I remember," Aunt Celia said to the crow. She smiled as she turned back to Jenn. "Familiars can be a blessing. They don't always do as they're told, however—but in Corvin's case it's usually for the best of reasons. He wants me to tell you a story to pass the time as we sort pages." She glanced back at the table and its disorganized assortment of paper. "It's a story about a dragon, a lonely girl, and a *very* naughty familiar."

The Hand of the Gorgon

Krimson, the crimson dragon, snoozed blissfully atop his glistening trove. He shifted slightly, setting off a tinkling of gold and jewels that echoed pleasantly across the stony cavern. Rays of noonday sun stretched through the distant natural skylight to warmly caress his scales. It was a day much like any other: calm, quiet, and solitary—exactly the way he liked it.

He preferred being by himself. He rarely received unwanted visitors anymore. The humans had long since stopped invading his home, their futile attempts to steal his precious treasures thwarted time and again with but a single, incinerating gout of flame. They had been slow learners. It had taken decades—and hundreds of telltale scorch marks—for them to realize he wouldn't tolerate such intrusion. He wanted to be left alone in peace, nothing more, nothing less.

Only the hunt for food or a refreshing dip in the sea could occasionally draw him from the depths of the long-extinct volcano he called home. On those excursions, he would do his best to avoid the humans, complete his objectives, and return to his sanctuary as quickly as possible. It wasn't that he feared them—their annoyingly sharp spears and arrows bounced off his thick scales far more frequently than they penetrated—but it was clear that they considered him the enemy, and he had little desire to participate in their foolish games of conquest and war.

No, it was far better to remain in isolation. By himself. Alone . . .

Tap, tap, tap.

Opening one eye, Krimson scanned the golden horizon, searching for the source of the sound. *What now?* he wondered.

His eye fell upon a familiar gilded mirror. It rested against an oversized figurine of the goddess Aphrodite, her shiny bare bosoms pointed skyward. Facing the dragon within the mirror's small oval reflection stood a crow, its beak rapping firmly against the far side of the glass.

Tap, tap, tap.

Not again, thought Krimson, as the bird peered back at him.

With a nod of recognition, the crow hopped forward, passing through the smooth surface and into the dragon's realm.

"Hello, my friend!" cried the crow cheerfully, struggling momentarily for purchase as several jewels and gold coins shifted beneath his feet.

"We are *not* friends," grumped Krimson in his deepest gravelly voice. "What brings you here on this day to disturb my rest?"

"I have the most urgent of favors to ask—"

"No. Absolutely not. Go home, Corvin. I told you not to use the looking glass to cross between our worlds again." The crow had a matching mirror—or so he'd claimed upon his previous visit—and the two were somehow connected to each other. The devices were quite useless for travel as far as Krimson was concerned. The one in his possession, at least, was absurdly small—nowhere near large enough for even a human to pass through, much less a magnificent being like himself. And besides, why would he ever want to leave his luxurious sparkling abode? He regretted not melting the mirror at his first opportunity.

"Don't be such a grump," said the visitor. "Someone's gotten up on the wrong side of the treasure heap!"

The dragon opened his eyes wide at the bird's scolding but Corvin, still studying the vast piles of riches, failed to notice.

"I've been thinking about our two lands," the crow continued. He skittered lightly over the tinkling mounds to stand in front of the dragon's huge snout. "Although our worlds do seem quite different, I'm wondering if they are not, in truth, one and the same—or were at one time, at least."

"I'm not sure I follow—and I don't think I care." Krimson was already growing tired of the conversation.

"Magick is significantly less common where I come from. In fact, the average person doesn't even believe it to exist. Dragons and other outlandish—er—wondrous creatures such as yourself are things of legend, certainly not to be found in twenty-first century Connecticut, or any other known place on the planet. And yet, even though our worlds seem so different, I can't help but notice the ancient Greek influences you have about the place." Corvin glanced upward, his gaze coming to rest upon Aphrodite's pert golden breasts. "The Greek mythos seems to be a theme common to both. Why do you suppose that is?"

"How should I know?" the dragon replied impatiently.

"Tell me, are you familiar with the creature known as the gorgon?"

Krimson thought for a moment, surprised by the question. He lifted his massive head several feet into the air. "Female? Snakes for hair? So vile that one gaze will turn a man to stone?"

"Yes, that's the one."

"Nope, never heard of it." He laid his chin back onto the heap. Wherever this conversation was headed, the dragon wanted no part of it.

The crow, however, seemed greatly relieved by the response, as if a tremendous weight had been lifted from his shoulders. "Thank goodness!" He hopped up and down excitedly. "You, my friend, are in a position to do me—and my world—a great service."

"And why would I want to do that?" His enormous brows knitted together. "And what happened to *you*?" The crow's stance had shifted and for the first time Krimson noticed that one of the bird's wings had been bandaged and immobilized within a large splint. Corvin had clearly been through a traumatic experience.

"To make a long story short, my companions and I have been fighting an evil necromancer by the name of Malleus Hodge. We'll soon have an opportunity to defeat him once and for all—but to do so will require an object we've had no hope of obtaining."

"And that is?" Krimson immediately regretted posing the question, but his curiosity had gotten the better of him.

"My mistress is a very powerful witch. She's located a banishing spell—but it requires a component that doesn't exist in our world. Despite my injuries and without her knowledge, I've come here hoping to obtain it: *the hand of a gorgon.*"

What? thought the dragon. *No. I'm done.* He again lifted his massive head. "You can go now. It's been a nice visit, but I have a nap to take. Please smash your mirror on the way out."

"We should leave at once. Time is very much of the essence." The bird clearly wasn't taking no for an answer.

"Are you seriously asking me to help you kidnap a snake-headed serpent lady who can turn people into solid rock?"

"No, you've gotten it all wrong. We don't need the whole gorgon—just one hand."

Sigh.

Corvin continued: "How often are you given the opportunity to take part in something so important—to get away from this gloomy cavern and journey far and wide—to demonstrate your power, strength, and magnificence!"

"Gloomy cavern?" Krimson raised an eyebrow.

"Well, it could use a bit of tidying." The crow scanned the piles of gold and jewels with a condescending shake of the head.

"No. Absolutely not." Krimson snorted black smoke. He had had enough. There was no way he'd ever take on such a foolhardy mission. "This conversation is *over.*"

"Have you put on weight?" asked Corvin. "You barely made it over the tree line."

"No, I haven't put on weight. Will you just stop talking?" Krimson soared through the sky toward the north, the crow perched on one shoulder, its claws buried deep in between the dragon's scales. Unable to fly due to his injuries, the bird had to be carried by Krimson. "How you ever talked me into this—I will never understand."

Fluffy white clouds dotted the blue sky. Banking slightly eastward, the dragon caught an updraft, his massive wings propelling them even higher into the air. Green hills and valleys soon spread out before them, stretching into the distance.

"And you've seen this gorgon?" Corvin asked. "You know where to find her?"

"I said as much, didn't I? It's been many seasons, however—there's no guarantee she's still there. And even if she is, she'll be unlikely to donate a hand to your cause."

"Let's cross that bridge when we come to it. For now, what can you tell me about her?"

"Only that she lives in a cave by the sea, the entrance to which is surrounded by scores of lifelike statues—statues that at one time had been living, breathing human men. While I have no love for humans, that fate seems particularly harsh—even to me."

"Humans aren't so bad."

"We'll have to agree to disagree."

As they continued their journey, Corvin shared with Krimson the story of Medusa, one of three gorgon sisters, who was beheaded by the Greek hero Perseus who then used her head as a weapon to turn his enemies to stone.

"Perseus had the help of the gods Athena and Hermes," replied the dragon. "We have no such aid. To my knowledge, no god has shown his or her face in this world during my long lifetime."

"The gods, of all varieties, have largely disappeared from my world as well."

The dragon continued northward for much of the afternoon. They passed over an ancient forest, the dense, gnarled foliage blocking any glimpse into its shaded interior. Gradually the trees began to thin, and the wooded area gave way to grassy plains. As the sun began to dip below the horizon, Krimson spotted a familiar human village. Beside the village rested a pasture, in which dozens of cattle grazed. Without warning, the dragon spiraled downward toward the field of cows.

"What—where are you going?" cried the crow. They struck the ground with a thunderous thud in the center of the nibbling bovines.

"It's been a long flight," replied the dragon. "I need to refuel. Beware the humans here—they're a particularly nasty lot."

Krimson let loose a torrent of flame, his breath washing over a patch of land dozens of square meters across. Corvin let loose a squawk as the flames died away, leaving behind a half dozen cows, still burning, wailing in agony as dragon fire burned away hair, skin and flesh. One by one they toppled, their charred corpses tumbling to the ground in silent death.

"Oh. My. GOD!" cried Corvin, fluttering off the dragon's shoulder as Krimson began devouring the smoking remains. "What have you done?"

"Help yourself—we haven't much time. The humans will be upon us shortly." The dragon wasn't used to sharing his meals, but under the circumstances it seemed the thing to do. Surprisingly, the crow didn't seem eager to share in his feast.

His loss.

At that moment, a spray of arrows shot past. Several others bounced harmlessly off his thick scales.

"What the holy *hell*?" cried Corvin amidst the shower of projectiles.

"Time to go," Krimson replied. Downing the final carcass, the dragon lowered his head, pausing long enough for the agitated crow to hop back on. As Corvin returned to his perch on Krimson's shoulder, the dragon leaped into motion. He felt the added weight of his meal as he lumbered away from the charging mob, his wings lifting them swiftly into the air and out of reach of the arrows.

They flew in silence for a time until the dragon spotted a winding river flowing far below. Gliding downward in a graceful arc, they came to rest on the northern bank where Krimson paused for a cool, refreshing, drink.

"You've been unusually quiet," the dragon remarked before releasing a thunderous belch. It was true. The crow's regular chatter had stopped since the encounter with the villagers.

After a moment, Corvin spoke: "I must say I found our previous stop truly horrifying . . ."

"Yes, I warned you. The humans—"

"No. Not the humans. You."

"Me? I—*what?*"

"The humans were just protecting their property. You dropped out of the sky and gruesomely laid waste to their cattle. What did you expect them to do as you sat there sloppily eating your ill-gotten roast beef?"

"What would you have me do?" A burst of anger filled Krimson at the bird's reaction. "They've attempted to steal my treasure for years."

"Perhaps they were just trying to collect recompense for *your* thievery!"

"WHAT?"

"Have you ever considered paying them for their troubles? You have heaps of treasure lying around just taking up space. Would it hurt you to give them a coin or two in exchange for food?"

"I—I suppose not." Krimson had never considered his actions from the humans' perspective. As much as he hated to admit it, the crow had a point. The dragon lowered himself to the ground, resting his chin on the riverbank. As the calm waters passed by, he considered Corvin's words. His eyelids grew heavy.

By this time, the sun had disappeared from the sky, making way for the moon and dozens of twinkling stars. The dragon and the crow spent the rest of the night in silence, dozing by the river's edge, each one dreaming restlessly of days past—and of days to come.

In the morning, Corvin was his former talkative self, and after a quick splash in the river, dragon and crow were once again in the air, heading northward.

"With your damaged wing," said Krimson, "you won't be of much help against the gorgon."

"That's true. I'm supposed to be on bed rest. But you'll still have the benefit of my considerable advice and knowledge."

Terrific—what could possibly go wrong?

By midmorning, they'd reached the ocean and had ventured out over the churning waves.

"Why aren't we sticking to the shoreline?" asked the crow.

"The land curves west here in a wide arc that turns back on itself further to the north. This is the most direct path to our destination."

As the blue waters passed below, Krimson thought about their journey so far. As much as he hated to admit it, he was enjoying the crow's company—and he'd learned some things about himself. Perhaps companionship had its benefits after all.

"Do you hear that?" asked Corvin a while later, breaking him out of his reverie. A series of cries could be heard off in the distance.

They soon came upon a ship, its sails unfurled, caught in what appeared to be a giant whirlpool. "*The Sea Spray*" was painted on its hull in fancy script. Humans dotted the deck and rigging. They moved about excitedly, trying to maneuver the massive sea vessel out of the churning vortex.

It was clear to Krimson that their efforts were failing.

"We have to help them!" cried Corvin. The dragon hovered a short distance from the maelstrom, his powerful wings adding to the water's turbulence.

"We must do no such thing—in fact it would be in our best interest to depart immediately." A sense of foreboding overtook the dragon. If he was correct—

"Krims, watch out!"

A large blue shape burst from the dark depths below them. What seemed like miles of scaled coils encircled Krimson's body, yanking him downward as he struggled to remain in the air. Salty ocean water filled his nostrils as he and the crow plunged beneath the waves. The dragon's wings struggled to propel him skyward. As he broke back through the surface, he caught a glimpse of his attacker and realized that his fears were well-founded.

Azure sea dragons were a crimson's worst nightmare—and Krimson's sudden appearance had interrupted this one's plan to sink the humans' ship. With powerful fins and serpentine bodies, azure dragons were comparable in both constitution and strength to the crimson. In their watery domain, however, sea dragons held the distinct advantage. And this one had Krimson in its coils.

In an attempt to free himself, he let loose a blazing lungful of dragon fire—which the sea dragon met with an equal exhalation of water. The resulting steam engulfed both dragons, impairing visibility. Krimson took the opportunity to bury his teeth into the nearest coil, causing the sea dragon to loosen its grip—and in moments he'd torn free. He soon realized, however, that the azure had simply changed tactics. With incredible speed, it swam circles around him, over and over, faster and faster, until the ocean fell in on itself, forming a funnel similar to the one that had nearly overtaken the humans' ship.

His body, circling uncontrollably within the vortex, his wings flailing uselessly, one in air, the other in water, Krimson found himself out of ideas. He had no way to extricate himself—the azure had him. He was tiring and before long, he knew, he would slip beneath the surface and lose consciousness. It would be the end of his journey and the end of Corvin's hope to—

"Corvin!" he cried, realizing the crow was no longer perched on his shoulder. He imagined the bird plummeting into the sea during the struggle with the azure. The despair he suddenly felt surprised him, causing his body to go limp, his struggling to cease. As his eyes scanned the maelstrom's interior searching for the crow, the water began to calm around him, and before he understood what was happening, the whirlpool was gone. Krimson found himself bobbing on the surface of the ocean, the three-masted ship floating nearby, the humans' attention focused solely on him. There was no sign of the crow.

Krimson took a moment to catch his breath. He knew the sea dragon's attack wasn't over. The azure likely believed him overtaken with exhaustion, which wasn't far from the truth—but he wasn't ready to give up just yet.

This time when the sea dragon broke the surface, Krimson was ready. He bathed the azure in flames before the other dragon had a chance to react. It screeched in pain, but didn't slow, and in moments it had once again wrapped its body around Krimson's. The azure's coils began to contract around him, like a boa constrictor around a rat. Unfortunately, this time the beast had trapped Krimson's wings against his body, which, along with the exhaustion, left him little chance for escape. The crimson dragon bobbed once in the water and began to sink below the surface. The sea dragon roared in victory as they sank, releasing a jet of water from its mouth in celebration, a horrific draconic fountain slowly disappearing into the depths.

Krimson suddenly felt his enemy's body tense, however, and realized something was amiss. He glanced skyward in time to see Corvin approaching from the direction of the ship. He was overjoyed to see him alive and well. The crow's splint was gone but his erratic trajectory demonstrated how unready he was for such flight.

Before he realized what the bird had in mind, Corvin landed on top of the azure's head, sinking his claws into the creature's right eye. The sea dragon wailed in agony as the crow's beak tore into its cornea, tossing away gory strip after gory strip. The coils around Krimson's body fell away as his adversary fought to attack the crow with its teeth, to no avail. Now free, Krimson bathed the azure's good eye in flame, turning it and the surrounding flesh to goo within seconds.

The blinded sea monster clearly realized it had lost. Screeching in anger, pain, and frustration, it sank into the depths, leaving Krimson, Corvin, and the ship full of humans floating on the open water.

"They cheered me," said Krimson as he and Corvin continued their journey northward, the calm blue waters passing serenely below them. "The humans actually cheered me."

"Well, you did save them from that horrible sea serpent." The crow had returned to his spot on the dragon's shoulder.

"I did, didn't I?"

"You did good, Krims."

Krimson felt his heart swell with emotion. "I thought I was done for."

"I knew there was no way that blue monstrosity could ever sink you."

"I *am* a deadly opponent, aren't I?"

"Yeah, that . . . and fat floats."

Within an hour, the coastline came into view to the northwest.

"It isn't much farther," said Krimson. "How's the wing?"

"Not great—but I think I'll live—unless we get turned to stone, that is." The bird twittered at his own joke.

"We should be fine as long as we don't look her in the eyes."

"Are you familiar with the story of Atlantis?" asked the crow, changing the subject.

"The lost sunken city?" The dragon turned his head to better hear Corvin's bird-speak over the wind.

"Yes, it's said that Zeus and the other gods allowed the island to be swallowed up by the sea—but that it is still, even today, a thriving metropolis in spite of its isolation."

"If you say so—why do you ask?"

"I've been wondering if your world could have been isolated from ours in a similar manner. It would explain some of our worlds' commonalities . . ."

"Perhaps."

They followed the shoreline northward until smooth sandy beaches gave way to stony cliffs. Soon a break in the rock face provided entrance to a small cove.

"This is it," said Krimson as he lowered his bulk into the water up to his shoulders. "We should remain hidden until ready to act."

"Agreed, my buoyant buddy."

"I am not your—" He cut himself short. Were they friends at this point? If not, then what were they? Dragons were not accustomed to having . . . comrades? Colleagues? Allies?

Corvin hopped onto the dragon's head as Krimson sank deeper until only his snout and eyes were visible. Slowly they entered the bay, moving as silently as possible toward the shore. Set back from the beach stood the entrance to a cave, surrounded on all sides by scores of standing stones that the dragon knew to be neither natural, nor manmade—they were gorgon-made.

"Are those—?" began the crow as the men's individual body parts and features became clearer.

"Yes," he whispered, lifting his mouth out of the water. "There are more than I remember seeing last time. We need to remain quiet."

No sooner had he lowered his head back into the water than he sensed movement from the mouth of the cave—it was she. It was the gorgon.

The creature exited her subterranean abode wrapped only in a cloth. She made her way toward the shore, pausing briefly to drop the makeshift towel on the sand. Writhing, hissing hair aside, she was gorgeous—for a human, at least:

well-toned and curvaceous, lovely facial features and beautiful skin. She'd have been a catch for any man, if not for her tendency to turn flesh into stone.

"Oh my," whispered Corvin.

What now?

"It would appear that serpent follicles aren't exclusive to the scalp . . ."

As the gorgon approached the waterline, her lower half transformed. Two legs became one, lengthening and coiling beneath her in the manner of a snake. Well-tanned skin gave way to scales, and by the time she entered the waves, she was pure viper below the waist. Slithering across the surface of the water like an anaconda, she splashed and frolicked as she bathed in the sea.

Krimson and Corvin waited and watched. The gorgon sang to herself, a sweet melody accentuated by the rhythmic buzzing of her ophidian hair, each strand dancing hypnotically in unison. Eventually she finished her dip and retreated back toward the beach.

Thank goodness, thought Krimson. *I couldn't have stayed submerged much longer.*

"Thank goodness," whispered Corvin. "Oh, shit!"

At that moment a rock came free from the closest cliff face. The dragon watched in horror as it tumbled through the sky in their direction, striking the water with an impossibly loud *plop*.

The gorgon's coif of writhing serpents turned toward them in unison, fangs bared and hissing—and the rest of her head turned, following suit.

Krimson ducked beneath the surface before the creature's gaze could fall upon him, hoping Corvin had done the same. Had she seen them? If so, the results could be disastrous . . .

When at last he chanced a peek back toward the cave, she was gone.

"That was close," whispered the crow, damp but unpetrified. "Let's find somewhere to dry off and plan our next move."

As quickly and soundlessly as possible, dragon and crow emerged from the water and took to the sky. The clifftop above the cave entrance had a good view of the beach and bay—and enough cover to prevent them from being seen from below. They rested at the cliff's edge for a time, and as the afternoon sun warmed damp feathers and scales, they discussed their next steps.

"I'm far too large to enter the cave," said Krimson. "We'll have to entice the gorgon to come outside."

"And then what?"

"You really didn't prepare for this moment, did you? We have no plans, no weapons, and no means to subdue her." *So much for the bird's considerable advice and knowledge.*

"Yeah, sorry about that. Been busy nearly dying . . ." The crow glanced at his wounded wing. He'd been favoring it even more since the encounter with the sea dragon. "I could enter the cave and check the place out, maybe find something that could help us."

"Yes, and get turned into the world's ugliest doorstop. With your bad wing, I don't think that's a good idea. She has us at a severe disadvantage—we're in her territory and we don't even have a safe way to look at her."

"Points taken."

"Perhaps we could drop this on her." Krimson sat up and with a large wing, pushed a nearby boulder to the cliff's very edge.

"Seriously?"

"Do you have a better idea?"

The crow appeared to think for a moment. "Boulder it is!"

At that moment, the dragon heard the ringing of a far-off bell. "Do you hear that?"

Corvin listened for a moment. "Yes—what do you suppose it means?"

They scanned the horizon and in moments spotted a ship nearing the mouth of the cove. Three masts sprouted from its wooden deck where a dozen humans scurried about like ants.

"Is that—?" continued the crow.

"Yes, I do believe it is." Krimson was surprised to see *The Sea Spray*, the ship they'd rescued from the azure dragon. "Here—in the gorgon's bay. What are the odds?"

"Surely they know the dangers of this place."

They watched in uncertain silence as the vessel moved shoreward, dropping anchor when it reached the inlet's center. A dinghy was lowered to the water with six men aboard. Wielding oars, they set off for the shore.

The rowboat ran aground on the sand, and the landing party exited the craft, wading through the shallow water and onto the beach. Five of the men wore red-and-black uniforms, long curved swords dangling from their waists. Plumed hats sat atop their heads, the feathers dancing in the ocean breeze.

The sixth man, however, appeared quite different. He wore the brown overalls of a laborer and was both hatless and weaponless. Krimson noticed immediately that his hands were secured behind his back. A pair of sailors led him forward, each grasping one of the man's arms.

"That one's a prisoner," Krimson said to the crow. "What do you suppose they have in store for him?"

"I think we're about to find out."

As the group of soldiers approached the mouth of the gorgon's cave, one of them stepped forward, his eyes focused on the ground.

"Queen Muffy of the Serpents," he called, "Mistress of Stone and Slayer of My Predecessor—it is I, Emperor Castorius of Hyperborea, and I request an audience!"

"Her name is—*Muffy*?" choked Corvin.

Krimson shrugged his massive shoulders.

"We bring your yearly offering," called Castorius. As soon as he said this, the prisoner began to struggle. One of his guards unsheathed a sword and held its point to the man's throat.

"They're giving him to the gorgon," said Krimson. "I told you humans were horrible creatures."

"Some are, perhaps," replied the crow. "But not all of them."

Krimson didn't reply. His attention returned to the scene playing out below them.

Another sailor stepped forward, placing a box of fabric and fruits at the cave's entrance. "She's coming," he said fearfully, returning hurriedly to his place behind the emperor.

The men tied strips of cloth over their eyes, blindfolding themselves—except for the prisoner, who glanced desperately about, searching for a means of escape.

The sound of hissing snakes preceded her. The gorgon stepped out of the cave to stand before the assembled men. She wore a simple yet elegant white gown that fell to her knees. Her "hair" had been parted and secured into ponytails that squirmed on either side of her head.

"My Lady," began Castorius, "as per our agreement, we provide our offerings. I pray that they will be to your liking. Gentlemen?"

The two guards stepped forward, their captive in tow.

Suddenly, the ropes securing the man's hands fell to the sand. Jerking free of his captors, he yanked one of their swords from its scabbard. The guards, apparently unwilling to remove their blindfolds, groped about uselessly, unable to lay hands on the escaping prisoner.

The man rushed forward, his attention focused on the one person responsible for his predicament. With great speed and a force born of desperation, he thrust the tip of the stolen sword downward, burying it into Emperor Castorius's back.

The emperor gasped and lurched forward, tumbling to the ground. The prisoner yanked the weapon free and turned to flee—only to come face-to-face with the gorgon. He raised the sword above his head, preparing to defend himself . . .

The instant their eyes met, the man's flesh turned to stone, the blood-soaked weapon locked in his petrified grasp.

"Damn it, not again!" the creature cried. Her hair broke free of the ponytails and darted angrily about.

The remaining sailors, sensing that something had gone wrong, lifted their blindfolds long enough to see Castorius lying before them, his blood staining the sand. Fleeing in terror, they scurried in all directions, bumping into each other, tripping, stumbling, and falling to the ground, as they ungracefully attempted to escape the gorgon's gaze.

"They've gone mad!" Krimson glanced at Corvin, who nodded from his spot at the edge of the cliff.

"Yes, I think we should—"

The bird never finished his sentence. A section of cliff gave way beneath the heavy boulder, taking it and the crow with it. Krimson looked on as the bird plummeted over the edge, his damaged wing flapping uselessly in the air.

"For the love of—" the dragon sighed. He knew what he had to do. *He'd* moved the boulder to the cliff's edge. Corvin's predicament was entirely his fault. Hopefully the crow's wings had functioned well enough for him to have survived the fall.

The crimson dragon wasted no time. He took to the air, soaring downward in an arc that curved back toward the cave opening. The sailors were nowhere to be seen. To his amazement, the fallen boulder had landed directly on top of Emperor Castorius's body. If the sword hadn't killed him, the monstrous stone certainly had.

The gorgon stood facing the flattened emperor. Krimson's eyes fell upon Corvin. The crow lay beside the boulder, unmoving, stunned by the fall.

The gorgon took a step toward the bird. Concerned for his friend, Krimson let loose with a deafening roar.

Corvin, suddenly alert, bolted upright.

The gorgon spun toward him, eyes wide, hair hissing.

Krimson exhaled a gout of flame that enveloped her, setting her clothes on fire and withering her venomous coiffure. As the inferno dissipated a moment later, however, their eyes met—

And the dragon dropped like the stone he'd become. He struck the edge of the shoreline with a splash and remained there, unmoving.

Krimson discovered that in death, although he could no longer see, somehow, amazingly, he could think. And he could hear.

Voices—many voices—became audible. He couldn't make out the words, but he knew they were there. The murmurings were soon accompanied by other sounds—the sounds of metal striking rock.

"Krims, are you in there? Can you hear me?"

It was Corvin—and not only was the crow still alive, but he realized that he himself must be too. Somehow, he'd escaped the full wrath of the gorgon's curse.

Dragons aren't that easy to kill, he thought.

The clanging sounds continued for some time until eventually he felt a crack in his stone prison. A sudden release in pressure allowed him to move slightly, to inhale.

"Krims, my porcine pal—we're coming for you."

The fresh flow of oxygen energized him. With every ounce of strength he could muster, he fought—he fought to breathe, to move, to live.

Suddenly, the rock encasing his body shattered, falling to the ground in a shower of pebbles, gravel, and sand.

He was free.

To his amazement, he was surrounded by the remaining sailors, their chipped and damaged swords in hand. They had freed him—they'd hacked at his stone prison with their weapons until it had crumbled away.

They'd done it for *him*.

"You saved us again, my Lord Dragon," said the nearest one. "We are forever in your debt."

"You saved us from the gorgon!" the others cheered.

The sailors knelt at his feet.

"All hail Krimson the Corpulent!"

"*Krimson the Corp*—that was your idea, *wasn't it*, Corvin?"

"Welcome back, Krims." The crow was once again perched on his shoulder.

The sailors praised and cheered the dragon for some time. When they were finished, the four men boarded the dinghy and rowed off toward the ship, never to return.

"So, what happened to the gorgon?" asked Krimson, realizing he'd forgotten her in the excitement. The two of them were relaxing in the sand at the edge of the water. "Is she dead?"

"Er, no—not exactly," replied Corvin.

"No?! What do you mean?"

"Gorgons aren't that easy to kill. She retreated to her cave. We thought it best for the humans to think her deceased."

"Okay, you're going to have to explain to me what the hell you're talking about!" The dragon lifted his head high into the air and eyed the crow.

"Yes, you deserve an explanation—wait here."

Krimson watched in confusion as the bird skittered off toward the cave and disappeared inside.

Moments later, he returned, the gorgon in tow. She paused at the entrance to her cave. A cloth sack had been placed over her head and cinched about her neck. Her hair seemed limp, silent, and unmoving beneath the cloth—the result of his dragon fire, Krimson suspected. She wore a fresh, clean, unburned gown.

"Krims, meet Muffy. Muffy—Krims."

"Happy to make your acquaintance," said the gorgon, peering at him through two slits in the sack.

"Uh, er . . . Likewise?"

"I'd like to thank you," she said, "for convincing the humans not to return. In all these years, they've been unsuccessful in finding me a mate—and I'm running out of space in my lagoon." She gestured toward the field of statues protruding from the sand.

As they talked, Corvin made his way back to Krimson, returning to his customary perch on the dragon's shoulder.

"You were looking for a husband?" asked Krimson.

"Yes, it gets lonely here in my cave." Krimson sensed a hint of sadness in the gorgon's voice. "When I ventured forth on my own, they got very upset. They promised to bring potential candidates to me—but no one has yet been able to survive my curse. No one until *you* that is."

"Hey, I sense an opportunity here," whispered Corvin. "She *is* kind of cute."

"Oh, *hell no*," he whispered back. "But this *does* give me an idea . . ."

"She certainly seems happy," said Corvin from his spot in front of the gorgon's cave. "Good on you!"

"Yes, it actually feels nice to have helped—to have helped them both."

Dragon and crow looked on as the gorgon and the azure dragon frolicked in the waves. The blinded sea dragon had mellowed since their last meeting, and his new handicap made him immune to the gorgon's curse.

"They can care for each other and keep each other company," said the crow. "And they'll be able to live happily in seclusion. All you really need is one good companion, after all."

Krimson and Corvin watched the couple for a while longer until, at last, they decided it was time to leave.

"It's a shame we failed in our mission," said the dragon, "but under the circumstances . . ."

"I agree," said the crow. "But there's not much to be done about it."

At that moment, they noticed the gorgon slithering up the beach. Her tail had transformed back into legs by the time she reached them. She still wore the sack over her head, exclusively for their benefit.

"I can't thank you enough," said Muffy. To his surprise, the happiness in her voice touched Krimson's heart. "Panagapi is wonderful. We truly enjoy each other's company. I'm indebted to you. You've changed my life! You must tell me how I can repay you for your kindness!"

"There's only one thing we need," said Krimson, looking at Corvin. "But I'm afraid you can't help us."

"Please, tell me what it is you seek." The sack over the creature's head shifted as she glanced back and forth between the dragon and crow.

Corvin shared his story, including his need for the gorgon's hand.

"Well, why didn't you say so?" the gorgon replied excitedly.

Hurriedly approaching her newest statue, she grasped the sharp, crimson-stained sword held firmly in its hand. With a quick tug, the weapon came free in a shower of stone fragments. Before Krimson could fully comprehend her intentions, the gorgon raised the weapon high into the air and brought it forcefully down upon her own wrist. The blade sliced through flesh and bone like butter. The severed hand hit the sand with a meaty plop.

"Muffy!" cried Corvin.

"How could you?" cried Krimson, stunned by her actions.

"What?" she said, staring at each of them through the eye slits in the sack. "They grow back . . ."

"You know, Emperor Castorius mentioned Hyperborea," said Corvin as they flew back toward Krimson's volcano, their grizzly prize safely secured. They were passing over the dark and gnarled forest they'd encountered on their journey north.

"Hyper-what?"

"Hyperborea. At first, I wondered if we were on the island of Thule, a lost land discovered by the fourth-century explorer Pytheas—but Hyperborea makes more sense. It was said to be a sunny land to the far north—a temperate, blessed place inhabited by those races favored by Apollo. The sun god must have locked your world away to protect it from the rest of the planet."

"Ha—I knew it! I'm one of Apollo's faves."

"Yes, you are, my friend."

Several hours later, the pair touched down on top of the dragon's immense pile of gold. Corvin hopped off the dragon's shoulder and fluttered to the ground. The treasure tinkled beneath his claws.

"Do you think you'll get the hand back in time?" asked Krimson. He flexed a muscle on his back, momentarily lifting one of his scales. The gorgon's severed appendage slipped free from its hiding place, landing with a plop beside Corvin. It already had a desiccated, aged appearance.

"Yes, I believe so. Time seems to pass slower in my world. I bet barely an hour has passed there."

"Best of luck."

"Thank you, Krims." The crow picked up the sickly-looking hand in his beak and hopped toward the magick mirror. He favored his injured wing. Krimson hoped that the journey hadn't caused it further damage.

"Uh, Corvin?"

The bird turned, pausing before the reflective surface.

The dragon lowered his snout and rested it beside the crow. "I, uh—if you ever need anything, or want to talk—I won't object to you returning here."

The crow nodded and disappeared through the glass.

Krimson felt truly sad to see him go.

This must be what friendship is all about, he thought.

He'd seen and learned so much in the last two days that he wouldn't have experienced if he'd stayed isolated at home, alone, in his treasure chamber. Companionship had its perks—and he remembered the rush he felt at receiving the humans' adulation. Perhaps the humans weren't so bad after all. Perhaps—

Suddenly, Krimson knew what he had to do. Grabbing several gold coins and jewels, the dragon took to the sky. He had a man to see about some cattle—and when he'd finished with that, there were other people and creatures to meet, to help, to rescue, and save.

The world needed him.

He was Krimson the Corpulent, after all, and he had a duty to fulfill.

JENN: PART II

Jenn glided down the street toward home, her feet resting on the bike's pedals. She coasted past Mr. Atwood's house, his freshly washed camper trailer out front, packed and ready for the first trip of summer. Next door, Mrs. Cortez's cat snuck stealthily through her flower garden, the bell on its collar tinkling a warning to any potential prey it might encounter. In the Fosses' yard, a sprinkler ticked, spraying water on nearly everything but the grass. Jenn chuckled to herself. She'd lived on this street her whole life, and nothing ever changed. Nothing ever surprised her.

The morning at the Watson house had been fun and informative. Jenn and Aunt Celia had sorted the bulk of the grimoire pages. Further collation and assembly were still required, however, and they had yet to discover how many of the old pages were missing. Although Jenn and Aunt Celia had talked at length on a variety of witchy topics, Jenn felt as though they had barely scratched the surface. Learning to be a witch was going to be an ongoing process, one that Jenn saw no reason to rush.

As she neared her own driveway, she noticed something unusual perched atop her mailbox. It appeared to be a large white bird. It sat there motionlessly facing the street, and for a moment Jenn wondered whether it was alive or stuffed—a living avian visitor or someone's handcrafted prank. Her curiosity aroused, she stopped the bike a few yards away and dismounted, leaning it momentarily against her leg. She removed her glasses and polished them on the hem of her shirt. Through clean lenses, she studied the mysterious bird. It resembled a great horned owl. The creature was over a foot tall, with prominent ear tufts sprouting from its head, but instead of the standard browns, grays, and blacks, this owl's feathers were as white as freshly fallen snow.

Jenn walked the bike cautiously over the curb, across the driveway, and toward the house. She set it down on the grass, her eyes never straying from the strange avian visitor. An unsummerlike chill raised the hairs on the back of Jenn's neck. The bird still hadn't moved, and for some reason, it gave her the creeps. Was it sleeping? Was it even alive? From where she stood, it looked very realistic, its plumage full and feathery—and yet it sat there like a statue. Jenn's heart began to beat rapidly as she stepped slowly toward it.

Suddenly, the owl's head snapped around to face her, its body still unmoving. Its gaze met her own. Jenn gasped, stumbling back in surprise. An inexplicable fear shot through her as the bird's large, unblinking orange eyes bore into her as if they had the ability to penetrate her soul.

Her heart racing, Jenn spun and ran for the front door. She struggled with her keys as she raced up the front steps. A peek over her shoulder revealed that the strange bird had also sprung into motion. Its wings spread wide, the owl turned toward Jenn, its large claws scraping the metal mailbox with a sound that made her skin crawl. The owl leaped into the air, its wings carrying it straight toward her—

Jenn's hands shook as she turned the key. She popped the front door open and slipped inside just as her pursuer touched down on the front stoop. The animal screeched, its chilling cry silenced as Jenn yanked the door shut behind herself.

What the hell? Jenn thought as she paused to catch her breath, her back pressed against the door. *Where did it come from, and what does it want?* Jenn turned the deadbolt, moved to a nearby window, and peered outside.

There was no sign of the giant snow-colored owl. Both the stoop and the mailbox were empty. The strange creature was nowhere to be seen.

Jenn glanced at her phone. Her parents weren't due home for several hours. Should she call someone? Maybe Zach or Nate or Aunt Celia? No, there was no need to bother them. She was just being silly—it was only a bird after all. Why then had the encounter disturbed her so? Jenn tried to put the experience out of her mind as she climbed the stairs to the second floor. She walked into her bedroom and sat on the bed. A collection of framed drawings lay arranged on the bedspread beside her, others scattered about the floor. Tomorrow was the Art Expo at the town library, and she still had some final preparations to complete. Jenn retrieved a large plastic tub from the floor and began placing the scattered drawings inside.

Later that night, Jenn bolted upright drenched in sweat. She'd had the dream again, the one in which she could fly. This time, however, the dream had soured, devolving from nighttime adventure to terrifying nightmare.

It began as it usually did—Jenn in her bedtime attire, soaring gracefully above her sleepy neighborhood without a care in the world, basking in the feelings of freedom and wonder that frequently accompanied her evening excursions through the treetops. She soon realized, however, that this time she'd been followed—pursued by the creepy white owl from the mailbox. It chased her through the night sky, its unnerving cries sending feelings of panic and despair coursing through her body.

Now, unable to sleep, Jenn lay back against her pillow. She could hear the crickets chirping outside her window. She picked up her phone and glanced at the time. It was just after four a.m. Jenn tossed the phone back onto her nightstand and closed her eyes, pulling the covers up over her head.

And that's when she heard it: a low moaning sound, like the howling of the wind. After a few seconds, it stopped. Jenn realized that the crickets had also gone quiet. She pushed the covers aside, swung her legs off the bed, and listened to the silence.

And then she heard it again:

Hoooooooooo

Jenn jumped up and moved to the window. Tossing the curtains aside, she peered into the darkness beyond, expecting to see nothing. What she saw terrified her. She swallowed hard as her heart dropped into her stomach.

Staring back at her through the glass was a pair of piercing orange eyes.

"I'm pretty sure the owl is stalking me," said Jenn into the cell phone tucked under her chin. She hurried down the stairs from her bedroom, the plastic tub of framed art in her arms. She was fully dressed and ready to leave the house. "It was waiting for me when I got home and then it spent the night perched in the tree outside my bedroom window."

"And you said it chased you in your dream?" asked Aunt Celia over the phone's speaker. By this time, Jenn had reached the front door. She set the tub of drawings on the floor.

"Yeah," she replied. "It freaked me out a little."

"It sounds strange, but I'm sure it's nothing to be concerned about," said Aunt Celia. "Why don't you come over after the Art Expo and we can talk more about it then?"

"Yes, I'll do that. Thank you."

"Of course," said Aunt Celia in a reassuring tone. Aunt Celia hung up the call from her end. With a sigh, Jenn slid the phone into her pocket and reached for the doorknob.

"Jenn, are you ready?" called Jenn's mother from the other room.

"Yeah, just give me a few minutes to put the stuff in the car," Jenn called back. She felt much better. Speaking with Aunt Celia had relieved her anxiety. Logically, she understood how silly she was being. It was just an owl, nothing more. Putting the night's troubles aside for the moment, she focused on the day ahead: friends, the Art Expo, and another visit with Aunt Celia.

Jenn pulled open the front door and was met with bright sunshine and a sour smell that knotted her stomach. When her eyes fell upon on the stoop, she recoiled in horror. Several small bodies, dotted with flies and clotting blood, lay drying in the morning sun. In the center, surrounded by a ring of expired mice and birds, lay an eviscerated rabbit, its one dead eye staring blankly skyward.

Something snapped in Jenn in that moment, fueled by frustration and disgust. She scanned the yard and the street before her, finding nothing unusual. She knew how the animal corpses had gotten there. It was clear that the ghoulish white owl was intent on tormenting her. The reasons behind it didn't matter—Jenn was done being frightened. If the bird wanted to wage a war of wits, then a war it would receive.

Machinations in Miniature

Courtney Stevens stood in the public library, applying the final touches to her art display. When she was done, she stepped back to admire her work and smiled. The presentation in front of her was nothing less than a masterpiece!

Her project featured an array of impeccable designer clothing, skillfully combined into a single perfect outfit: a slate-gray, single-breasted jacket and midi skirt by Prada, gently laid over the back of a chair, a simple white Ralph Lauren broadcloth shirt tucked inside. A pair of black Louis Vuitton calf-leather pumps rested on the chair's seat. Beside the shoes, she'd placed the pièce de résistance—a scarlet envelope-style purse, embossed with Vuitton's signature monogram pattern. Every piece of clothing looked flawless, and when combined, the ensemble was to die for—true art in its finest form.

Her only regret was not having a better way to display the garments. She'd asked Ms. Brooks, the school librarian in charge of the Expo, to supply her with a proper dress mannequin for the event. It was the least she could do, after all, since Courtney would be providing the expensive designer wardrobe.

"The high school can't afford to rent you a full-scale dummy, Courtney," the librarian had said. "We're already over budget as a result of the auditorium fire. With the school closed for repairs, we're fortunate that the town library was able to host us free of charge—but I'll see what I can come up with for you."

After the fire at the school, the year-end final exams had been canceled and the students released early for summer vacation. Normally, Courtney would have been thrilled by either of these eventualities, but truth be told, Courtney was relying on her finals to help boost her GPA. It had been a difficult year, and she was in danger of not graduating. When she learned of the art show and that Ms. Brooks had opened it up to anyone in need of a little extra credit, Courtney was both relieved and excited.

Unfortunately, in the end, Ms. Brooks failed to come through with the mannequin, or any other means of displaying Courtney's finery—save for a single lousy, dinged-up chair. Even so, Courtney wasn't worried. Her project was far and away better than those of the other students—of that she was certain.

Twirling a strand of blonde hair around her finger, she glanced around the room. Tables had been brought into the library's large conference room and placed around its perimeter. Many of them contained student projects in various stages of completion. In the center, suspended from the ceiling, hung a banner with the words "What Does Art Mean to You?" in large letters.

Jenn Quigley stood nearby arranging the most confusing assortment of framed black-and-white drawings Courtney had ever seen. She walked over to the table for a closer look. There were images of repeating puzzle-like sketches of interconnected angels and demons, fish and birds. One depicted a pair of hands sprouting off the page, each one drawing the other with a pencil. Yet others showed impossible buildings that made Courtney dizzy, with stairs that shot off in all directions.

"Hi, Jenn," she said.

"Hi, Courtney," Jenn replied with a smile, looking up from her display.

Courtney had purposely refrained from commenting on Jenn's bewildering collection of art. She'd realized that it was sometimes better *not* to verbalize the first thing that popped into her head. This took no small effort on Courtney's part—as a cheerleader, and one of the popular girls at school, she was unaccustomed to having to censor what she said. After the recent loss of her two best friends, however, Courtney had been soul-searching. She wanted to better herself, and that included being more considerate of other people's feelings.

At the table next to Jenn's was Zach Greenwood. His display consisted of an old boombox and a heap of CDs, most with cracked cases. Courtney's brows furrowed as she approached his presentation.

"What's that supposed to be?" she asked, her hands on her hips. "I mean, it looks like the leftovers from a bad garage sale. Who even uses compact discs anymore?"

Zach frowned, looking up from his arrangement of CDs. "Thanks, Courtney," he replied, glancing at Courtney's table. "I love yours, too. What do you call it, 'Laundry on a Chair'?"

No need to be rude, she thought, irritated by Zach's response.

"Everyone appreciates art differently," Jenn interjected, trying to calm the exchange of words.

"Yep, I enjoy music." Zach nodded, gesturing toward the boombox. "You like paintings and stuff—and Courtney likes . . . er . . . clothes?"

"Designer clothes," said Courtney. "They're the ultimate in artistic creativity and expression."

"I'll have to take your word on that," replied Zach, one brow raised.

At that moment, Nate Watson entered the library with Mr. Black, Courtney's biology teacher. Between them they carried what appeared to be a large brick dollhouse of Victorian style. Three square feet at its base, it stretched three stories tall with a wraparound, pillared porch. Large windows, topped with stained-glass transoms, traversed the lower two floors. A flat railed-in area sat atop the third, surrounded on all sides by sloping roof segments covered in miniature slate shingles.

"There you go, Nate," said Mr. Black as they set the intricate building down with some effort on the nearest free table.

"Thanks for the assistance, Mr. Black. I couldn't have done it alone. Marc was supposed to help, but he was nowhere to be found. You know how brothers can be."

"Any time, Nate," the teacher responded. "Hello, folks." Mr. Black nodded at the other students in turn, pausing a moment to look quizzically at Courtney's display before turning to Jenn's. "Ah, Maurits Cornelis Escher," he said at last, examining the framed artwork. "His pieces are fascinating."

"Yeah," said Jenn with a grin. "I love the optical illusions and patterns. They're quite unique."

"Agreed." Mr. Black nodded his approval.

The biology teacher said goodbye and left the room. Courtney returned to her display as Jenn and Zach joined Nate around the miniature structure. She pretended to make adjustments to her display as the three friends examined the tiny Victorian building.

"A dollhouse?" asked Zach. "Hey, this thing is sick!" When Courtney glanced toward them, Zach was bent over, peering through the first-floor windows. "The details are amazing," he continued. "Is that furniture in there?"

"Yeah, it's actually a scaled-down *model*," replied Nate. "I thought it would be a great representation of artistic architecture for the Expo."

"It *is* artistic," began Jenn, running her fingers along a row of miniature bricks. "It's a replica of your house. Where did it come from?"

"I thought it looked familiar," said Zach as he stood upright.

"Marc and I found it behind a pile of junk in the cellar." Nate shrugged. "I mentioned it to Aunt Celia. She thought it was probably left by the architect who designed the mansion."

Courtney continued watching and listening. She envied the trio's friendship. Courtney had recently helped them defeat the evil warlock, Malleus Hodge, in the old town graveyard. Her friend Kam hadn't survived the encounter, and her friend Kat had been ghosting her ever since.

"Want to get some lunch?" asked Zach. He glanced at Courtney, catching her gaze before she could avert her eyes. "You're welcome to join us, Courtney . . . if you want." Without waiting for a response, Nate, Jenn, and Zach turned and headed out of the conference room. Jenn and Zach were holding hands.

For someone used to being popular, Courtney hadn't been feeling very wanted lately. The invitation felt like a lifeline. She started after them, pausing as she passed the miniature mansion.

The detailed representation on the table before Courtney took her breath away. A far cry from the die-cut plywood dollhouses that populated many girls' bedrooms, this one was of top-notch construction—even better, she had to admit, than the one her parents had given her as a child.

The intricate elements were extraordinary. Tiny flecks of paint seemed to be flaking from the porch's white pillars, and a realistic wear pattern could be seen on the gray floorboards leading to the front door's rustic welcome mat. The outer walls appeared to be constructed of genuine mortared bricks. Tiny cobwebs, complete with trapped insects, decorated the slats of several of the window's shutters, and the slate-covered roof was made of actual tiny stone shingles. It appeared perfect in every way—more than perfect.

Courtney glanced through several of the windows, wondering if the inside was as detailed as the outside. Unfortunately, she was unable to see far into the darkened interior. The structure appeared to lack the common hinged feature that allowed most dollhouses to open wide. If the house *could* be opened in some manner, its seams were masterfully hidden with no obvious mechanism to gain entry.

Her eyes scanned the mansion with fascination—and a touch of jealousy. Nate may have done it—he may have actually surpassed her designer display with this impeccable sample of miniature architecture. He may have—

Courtney did a double take, her focus returning to a single gabled dormer window on the third floor. A light shone from within—a light she was certain had not been there moments before. She examined the window with interest, noting the dark paneled woodwork she glimpsed through its panes. Unfortunately, the house was too tall, the window over her head, making it impossible to obtain a direct view inside.

Grabbing a nearby chair, Courtney dragged it to the table, setting it before the towering dollhouse. She climbed onto the seat, excitedly preparing herself for a peek into the mansion's interior. Adjusting her posture so that her eyes were level with the window, she leaned forward for a better view—and what she saw inside sent chills through her body, causing her to nearly lose her balance. Only quick reflexes prevented her from tumbling off the chair.

A pair of eyes stared back at her—miniature eyes, set into a miniature face—a human face. She knew instantly the visage before her belonged to no doll. The features were too perfect: the eyebrows and eyelashes, the nostrils and teeth. Everything was flawlessly accurate and in proportion. The boy peering at her through the glass was a living, breathing, mini human being—and if any lingering doubt of his humanity remained, it instantly evaporated when the boy, eyes widening at being discovered, ducked out of sight.

Courtney, suddenly light-headed, stepped down from the chair.

Whoa, what the hell . . . ?

It was then that she noticed the small doorbell mounted beside the front door. It glowed an eerie crimson that was impossible to miss—and yet she hadn't seen it when she'd first examined the front porch. Had one of the large pillars obstructed her view? Or had the button only *now* begun to shine?

She looked back at the third-floor window. The lamp inside had been extinguished. For a moment, she wondered if she'd imagined the light—and the miniature boy—but the gleaming button reassured her that she hadn't. The doorbell called to her, its glow tempting her, beckoning her—

Passing her hand beneath the porch's overhang, she extended her index finger and pressed the tiny button, blotting out its crimson aura. She felt its slight movement, followed by a sound . . .

Ding—

Instantly, all of Courtney's senses short-circuited, her vision blurring as her stomach twisted in upon itself. She felt her heart begin to race.

Oh my god, what did I just do?

In a dizzying spiral of confusion, nausea, and growing weightlessness, Courtney's world turned black . . .

—Dong

It took Courtney a moment to regain her senses. Her swirling vision soon came back into focus to the great relief of her roiling stomach. She found herself inside a large foyer. Straight ahead, a grand staircase led up to the second floor. Intricate oak woodwork, stained a dark brown, stretched off in all directions—from the baseboards to the crown molding that ran along the ceiling.

Where was she? Was she dreaming? Had she fallen from the chair in the library and struck her head? Anxiety filled her as she contemplated the many unknowns.

Off to the left, Courtney discovered a partially opened pair of sliding doors. With a little effort, she pushed one of them to the side until it had fully retracted into the wall, allowing passage into an immense living room full of antique furniture. A fireplace sat against the room's far wall, a built-in bookcase adorning one side. Large windows traversed the long wall in front of her, topped with panes of colorful stained glass.

Stained glass?

Courtney hurried, unsteadily, across the hardwood floor toward the nearest window, afraid of what she might find on the other side. Shoving an old wooden chair out of her way and resting both palms on the sill, she gazed through the glass—and out past the large, white-trimmed covered porch.

Oh shit . . . How could this be?

She was dismayed, but not entirely surprised by what lay beyond. A large conference room scattered with tables stretched out before her. On one of the tables sat a familiar display of designer clothing, although now it appeared large enough to fit the Jolly Green Giant. Never in her life was she so horrified to see such a brilliant collection of Prada, Lauren and Vuitton—but their existence left no room for doubt. Either Courtney had entirely lost her mind—or she'd been reduced to the size of a gerbil and trapped within the miniature mansion.

Wait, she thought. Am *I trapped?*

Courtney unlocked the sash and rattled the window. As expected, it refused to open. Hurriedly, she retraced her steps to the foyer and retracted the front door's deadbolt. The door remained unmovable. She tried several other windows and was unable to budge any of them. It was clear that the house wasn't going to let her depart via any normal means. It then occurred to her that maybe that was for the best—if she didn't leave the same way she'd arrived, what would happen once she exited the building? Would she stay small? She had no desire to remain miniaturized. What use would the world have for a pocket-sized cheerleader? And where would she find appropriate clothing to wear?

Courtney suddenly remembered the boy she'd seen in the third-floor window. She wasn't alone in the mansion. Did he represent a danger? Or had he too become trapped in this miniature house of horrors? Gathering her wits, Courtney grabbed a brass candlestick from a nearby table, hefting it in her hands like a club.

This will have to do. Her first priority was to search the building for a means of escape. If she ran into the boy—or any other threat—well, it was best to be prepared for the worst. She climbed the main stairway to the second floor and began entering room after room. Each appeared very similar to the next: hardwood floors with fancy throw rugs, tall ceilings, fireplaces with elaborately carved mantlepieces, antique furnishings with comfortable-looking, quilt-covered beds . . .

One room stood out from the others, however. A combination showplace and workroom, it contained the strangest assortment of items she'd ever seen. Shelves and glass-fronted cabinets displayed crystals, books, and ancient devices of unknown purpose. A worktable full of beakers and other tools she recognized from her chemistry class sat along one wall beneath a forest of dried herbs suspended from the ceiling on strings. A pentagram, enclosed in a circle, had been painted on one wall. A large empty birdcage sat on the table beneath it.

The place gave Courtney the creeps. She stood there for a moment, her eyes traveling the room. It had all the components of a witch's workshop—the only thing missing was an old straw broom. *What is happening to me? This is insane.*

And not at all the day I had planned for myself. Feeling a bit unnerved, Courtney turned and ran out of the room—

—and came face to face with the boy she'd seen through the third-floor window. He was tiny no more—at least in relation to her own reduced size. He stood slightly taller than Courtney, his brown hair mussed, his clothing stained with fresh dirt and cobwebs. Her heart pounding in her chest, she brandished the candlestick at him in a threatening manner.

"Stay back!" she cried. "Who are you, and what are you doing here?"

"I—I live here," he replied, his palms raised in a don't-hurt-me gesture. "Well, sort of, anyway—and you *know* me, Courtney. We've met. Don't you remember?"

"I—er—wait, what?" Courtney lowered the candlestick and studied his features, a perplexed expression on her face.

"We've met—I'm Nate's brother . . . Marc. Don't you remember? The whole crazy thing at the cemetery? When we defeated the evil warlock, Malleus Hodge?"

Nate's brother? Marc's voice droned on in the background as Courtney worked through the situation in her mind. The boy did resemble Nate. He must have been trapped here just as she'd been. If he was familiar with the house and everything inside it, then maybe they could work together to find a means of escape.

"—you really don't remember me?" Marc was still speaking when Courtney slipped out of her reverie.

"I—well, I can't be expected to remember *everyone* I meet, can I?" Her voice betrayed her growing frustration. *There was a lot happening that day.*

"No, I guess not," he said softly, eyes downcast.

Feeling guilty for Marc's disappointed expression, Courtney changed the subject. "How did you get here?"

Marc raised his eyebrows. "I'd guess the same way you did. I was waiting for Nate this morning. It was almost time to leave for the Expo when I noticed the house's doorbell had begun to glow."

"And so you pushed it?" she asked. "And you've been stuck here all morning?"

Marc nodded, eyes wide. "Yep, I've been searching the house for anything out of the ordinary—it's an exact duplicate of our home, every detail. The pajamas I wore last night were on the bedroom floor where I dropped them in the real world—and the bowl I used for breakfast is sitting in the kitchen sink!"

Strange, she thought, *but not helpful in the least.* "Other than that, you found nothing unusual?"

"Well, not exactly—I did find this . . ." Marc pulled something from his rear pocket and pushed it into Courtney's face. It was a small doll, slightly larger than his hand—and it looked remarkably like him, down to the gray t-shirt and jeans he wore.

"Is this supposed to be you?" Courtney squinted at the cartoonish figure in the boy's hand.

"Dunno." Marc shrugged, shoving the doll back into a pocket. "Maybe. But this wasn't the only thing I found. Come, I'll show you."

Marc dashed past her and down the hallway. Courtney's mouth dropped open in surprise. "Hey, wait!" she cried, running after him. When Marc reached the front staircase, he hurried down it, two steps at a time. She did her best to catch up, but he was too fast.

I never agreed to this, she thought, pausing at the bottom of the stairs to catch her breath.

Courtney walked across the foyer and into the living room. Marc stood before the large fireplace.

"Dude!" he cried, pointing excitedly at the mantlepiece. "Look!"

"I'm *not* a dude." Courtney knit her brows.

"I mean, check it out—it's changed!"

Courtney approached, examining the shelf above the fireplace. On it sat a ghoulish-looking device from the seventeenth century—a pair of miniature nooses hung suspended from a wooden crossbeam, resting on two vertical supports.

"Your aunt has some creepy lame-ass décor," she said, wrinkling her nose at the disturbing decoration.

"It's called a gallows—and I've never seen it before today. What's weird is that before you arrived, there was only one noose!"

Courtney reached up, grasping one of the ropes. She gave it a tug and watched as the noose descended a few inches before stopping. When she released it, it returned to its original position, retracting like a person sucking down spaghetti.

"What do you think it means?" she asked.

"No idea."

"Well, you sure are helpful," she said, letting her irritation show. She frowned. One look at Marc's face and she instantly regretted her tone. "I—I didn't mean that," she continued, coming as close to an apology as her dignity allowed. "Now tell me, why would your aunt give Nate a dangerous booby-trapped playhouse with built-in shrink-ray?"

"Aunt Celia didn't know it was dangerous."

Great, she thought, closing her eyes, not sure whether to believe him. Her brain hurt. Nothing made sense—the miniature mansion, their entrapment, the odd device on the mantle, the ugly little voodoo doll of Nate's brother . . . Suddenly, an idea formed in her mind.

"Hey," she cried, opening her eyes and extending a hand. "Give me that doll."

Marc shrugged, retrieving the small cloth figure from his back pocket and placing it in her hand. Taking it, Courtney approached the device, carefully slipping one of the nooses around the doll's neck . . .

"Hey, what are you doing?" he exclaimed.

She let the miniature representation of Marc drop. The rope extended as it had before, but this time it stayed that way. The figure bounced at the end of the cord for a moment before she heard it—the sound of a bell.

Ding.

It was an abbreviated version of the mansion's doorbell, but to Courtney it was the ring of congratulations, a chime of success.

"Brilliant!" said Marc. "Horrifying, but brilliant—I didn't think of that! It's gotta be the secret to getting out of here!"

Courtney glanced at the young man and smiled, the compliment momentarily overriding her sour attitude. She couldn't remember the last time she'd received such an affirming reaction to anything. She returned her gaze to the mini gallows.

"You said there was only one noose before my arrival—and now there are two. Maybe the display has to be completed before it will release us. How did you find your doll?" If the mansion had created a figure in Marc's image, it made sense that somewhere there'd be one in hers.

"There was a riddle—it didn't help though. I *assumed* it was for the doll." He pulled a wrinkled piece of paper out of his pocket. On it were written the words:

Find me: I lift, pitch and tune, and with force, I can wound.

Courtney thought for a moment. *Lift . . . Pitch . . . Tune . . .* "Could the answer be *fork*?" she asked. "You know, like: *fork* lift, pitch *fork*, tuning *fork . . .*"

"You're a genius!" he cried excitedly. "I found the doll in the kitchen—in the silverware drawer. It's where we keep the forks!"

Courtney smiled. *This kid is okay,* she thought. She'd never been called a genius before—and his excitement was infectious. "Where did the riddle come from?"

"Oh, funny story," he laughed. "I found it in my *pants.*"

"Huh? But how—?" Courtney slipped her hand into the pocket of her jeans, and—much to her surprise—her fingers closed around a small slip of paper where her cell phone should have been. She pulled it out.

"Of all the nerve . . ." she said, somewhat troubled by the assault on her person. Brushing off feelings of indignation, she read the note aloud:

Find me: I enable movement by blocking movement.

I can mush, slush and crush.

"What's the answer?" asked Marc enthusiastically, as if expecting her to have the solution at the tip of her tongue.

Courtney thought for a moment. "The *hell* if I know . . ." she replied.

Jenn, Zach, and Nate entered the meeting room to find several students putting the final touches on their art projects. They made their way to Courtney's clothing display, which appeared just as it had before lunch.

"What do you suppose happened to Courtney?" asked Zach. "Is her art display finished?"

Nate shrugged. "I guess it must be," he said.

"Jeesh," said Zach, shaking his head at the chair full of garments.

It is *an odd interpretation of art,* thought Jenn. *Leave it to Courtney.*

Nate brushed a strand of brown hair from his eyes. "To each his or her own, I guess. Listen, there's not much more I can do with my display. I'm going to check out a book or two while you guys finish up."

"Actually, mine's done too," said Zach. "I'll come with, unless you need some help, Jenn?"

"You guys go ahead," she said with a shake of the head. "I'll be along in a few."

It wasn't until after the boys left the room that Jenn's eyes settled upon Nate's miniature mansion—and the tiny, glowing red button mounted beside its front door . . .

"We've searched for over two hours, and we've found nothing," said Courtney, dropping into a cushioned antique chair in the living room. She glanced irritatedly at the smudges covering her hands and clothing. "Doesn't your aunt ever clean around here?"

Marc shrugged, pulling up a chair by the windows.

"And what a useless clue," she pulled the crumpled slip of paper from her pocket. "'I enable movement by blocking movement'—how is that even possible?"

"That's how riddles work—they don't usually make sense at first." Fatigue was evident in the boy's voice.

Courtney sighed. *I know that,* she nearly snapped at him. Instead, she struggled to calm herself. Marc didn't deserve her anger. He seemed to look up to her, respect her even. He appreciated her for herself, not for the image she presented to the world. Taking a deep breath, she glanced back down at the paper. "'I can mush, slush and crush.'"

"I really thought we'd find the doll in the blender," said Marc.

Courtney laughed, giving him a smile. "It was a good guess." Marc returned a grin.

"So now what?" he asked.

"I guess we start our search again." She saw no other option. She stood and attempted to brush some of the grime off her favorite pair of jeans.

"Er, Courtney?" There was an alarmed tone to his voice.

She looked up to see him rising from his seat, his attention focused out the window.

"I think we have a problem," he said.

The monstrous hand filled the gap between the porch's floor and overhanging roof, its giant index finger at the ready.

"She's going to press it," said Marc as he and Courtney watched through the living room window. "Jenn's going to press the doorbell. She'll become trapped like us."

"That girl could use a good manicure," Courtney replied, "and some tweezing wouldn't hurt." Jenn's large brown eyes and eyebrows were visible on the horizon as she stooped to examine the glowing button.

"We should try to stop her," said Marc excitedly. "If she gets stuck in here, we'll probably get another noose and riddle."

The boy was absolutely right. The last thing they needed was another misleading clue and wild goose chase. She began banging on the glass. Jenn looked around, startled, but failed to glance in their direction.

"I don't think she can see us," he said, knocking rapidly on the glass with his knuckles.

Courtney remembered how difficult it'd been to view the inside of the house until Marc had illuminated the upstairs room. "It's too dark! We should turn on a light—"

Before they could act, however, Jenn stood and pulled back her hand. The girl stepped away from the house but remained facing them. They could no longer see her face. Only the lower half of her flowered blouse remained visible.

"We should go upstairs," said Courtney, "to a room she can see. If we can get her attention, maybe she can help us get out of here."

"Great idea."

They ran out of the living room, through the foyer, and up the grand staircase. Once on the second floor, they selected a room facing the center of the library and approached the window. Jenn stood a short distance away, carefully studying the mansion with her eyes, a perplexed expression on her face.

"Marc, get the light."

The boy turned and headed for the light switch. The instant he depressed the on button, they had Jenn's attention. The girl focused her gaze on their window as Courtney began banging on the glass. Marc joined her a moment later, adding to the noise with his fists.

Jenn approached the window, her eyes growing wide the instant she spotted them. Under any other circumstance, Courtney would have found her reaction comical. The girl's mouth dropped open, and she stumbled backward as Courtney and Marc jumped up and down, waving their arms, shouting at the top of their lungs.

"We did it!" cried Courtney. "She saw us—she . . . What the *hell?!*" Before their eyes, Jenn turned and ran out of the conference room—taking their best hope of rescue with her. Courtney glanced at Marc, unhappy to say the least. "Where does she think she's going?"

Marc, obviously disappointed, shrugged. "I'm sure she'll be back. I, uh, hope."

So now what? Courtney let out a long breath as she struggled to think. Other students were milling about the conference room. She realized it was only a matter of time until one of them approached the mansion.

"We should turn out the light," she said. "We don't want to attract anyone else's attention until we figure out what to do."

Leaving Marc by the window, she turned, heading for the switch. She pushed the off button, returning the bedroom to its darkened state. At the base of the room's door, she spotted a cast-iron doorstop in—of all things—the shape of a pig. Its presence sent chills through Courtney's body.

Her terror of pigs had begun at the age of six, during a school field trip to a local farm. While climbing a fence to view some nursing piglets, she'd fallen into the pen—right on top of the snoozing mother. Covered in mud, Courtney was chased around the enclosure by the squealing creature until a farmhand wrangled it into a corner of the pigsty so that she could escape.

Courtney relived the horrible experience in her mind: the mud, the screeching animal, the laughter of the other kids. It'd been a true nightmare, a horrific—

Suddenly, it dawned on her—the riddle! 'I enable movement by blocking movement.' The farmhand had blocked the pig, allowing *her* to flee the pen! Excitement filled her. She reached for the doorstop, hefting the heavy piece of cast iron in her hand. She was certain she'd solved the riddle and proud of herself for having done so.

"I can *mush*, *slush* and *crush*!" she cried, bringing the metal animal down into her open palm, as if to emphasize each word. "You could *kill* someone with this thing!" She turned to Marc, grinning and eager to share her reasoning with him.

"You did it! You solved the riddle!" he said excitedly. "I never doubted for a *minute* that you'd figure it out!"

"Yeah, it was simple really—when I was six—"

"A doorstop *blocks* the movement of a door, *enabling* people to move through it! You're a freakin' Einstein!"

Courtney frowned as she processed Marc's words, realizing with disappointment that *he*—and not she—had in fact solved the puzzle. The boy, oblivious to the blow he'd struck her ego, approached the door, yanking it away from the wall. There on the floor rested a well-dressed doll with long blonde hair. He picked it up and handed it to her.

"This is all wrong." she said, studying the object before her. "My hair is *not* this stringy . . ." She turned the figure over in her hand. "And my ass isn't—"

"OH, NO!" Marc's exclamation broke her train of thought. Nervously, Courtney turned to see what had alarmed the boy.

Through the window, she saw Jenn, who'd returned with the boys. Nate and Zach stood on either side of her, their hands resting on her shoulders. As one, the three of them bent at the waist until only the tops of their heads were visible, their attention focused on the mansion's front porch and door—and very likely, on the malevolent glowing button.

"Quick! To the living room," cried Marc, running past Courtney at full speed.

She hurried after him, the ugly doll grasped in her hand. The boy was right—their only hope was to place the figure in the display before some idiot pressed the evil glowing doorbell. They had an opportunity to escape the miniature mansion now, but only if they were quick enough to beat—

Ding—

"*Nooo!*" Courtney screamed from the top of the grand staircase as she felt her heart drop into her stomach. They were too late.

Fantastic, she thought.

—Dong

Just freakin' fantastic . . .

"Courtney's a genius," said Marc excitedly. "She nearly had us out of here—would have in another five minutes."

"Are we talking about the same—" began Zach. Jenn discretely elbowed him in the stomach before he could say anything further.

The five of them stood before the living room fireplace, examining the horrific display. The figures of Marc and Courtney hung from the two original nooses. Three new ones hung empty beside them. Marc had filled the others in on the gallows, the dolls, and the riddles—and sure enough, when each of the newcomers had reached into his or her pocket, there'd been a fresh riddle waiting to be solved.

"We need to find the missing dolls," continued Marc, "before the rest of the library is locked in here with us!"

"Let's do this, then," said Nate. Jenn and Zach nodded in agreement. Courtney, for her part, had remained silent since the appearance of the others, partly out of frustration, partly to avoid conflict. The preceding hours had taken a lot out of her, and she wasn't sure she'd be able to contain her sarcasm.

"I'll start," said Zach, reading his riddle out loud:

Find me: I reveal words with a slice; no need to ask twice.

"Courtney?" asked Marc hopefully. Everyone turned to look at her.

"I, er . . ." Courtney was at a loss. One of her biggest fears was looking stupid in front of others, and Marc had put her on the spot. She struggled to think. *'I reveal words,' it said. Words are made up of letters.* "Something to do with letters?" she said at last, cringing inside.

Marc thought for a moment. "That's it!" he cried. "A letter opener—it slices open envelopes—and there are words inside every letter!"

"Wow . . . Nice job, Courtney." Zach gave the compliment, sounding truly impressed.

Did that really just happen? thought Courtney. She found herself smiling.

Marc hurried into the foyer, the others in pursuit. A table stood against one wall, several pieces of mail resting on top. He pulled open a small drawer, revealing a sharp brass letter opener—and a cloth replica of Zach, a mop of sprawling dark hair sprouting from its scalp and a goofy grin on its face. Courtney fought to suppress a laugh. Zach's doll was even worse than her own.

"Okay, Jenn," said Marc. "Your turn."

Jenn read hers aloud:

Find me: One way or two, I'll alter your view.
My shard is fierce; your throat it'll pierce.

"Is it just me," Jenn continued, a look of concern on her face, "or are all these clues very violent?"

Courtney thought of the magnifying mirror she'd broken on Saturday while applying her makeup. One of the broken pieces had sliced open her finger, bloodying the countertop. It was sharp enough that it could've easily pierced someone's throat. "Is it a mirror?" she suggested with growing confidence.

The others nodded their agreement. Her solution made sense.

"A mirror can be one-way or two-way," summarized Marc. "And everything you see in them is reversed! Courtney did it again!"

Maybe I'm good at riddles after all, thought Courtney with increasing pride. *Or at least I don't* totally *suck!*

The group searched the house for mirrors, and in the second bathroom, they found the one they were looking for. Jenn's doll, curly brown hair splayed about its shoulders, sat inside the medicine cabinet beside an old straight razor and a bar of soap.

Nate's riddle came last:

Find me: Take a step if you dare.
I'll introduce you to air.

Out of habit, they all turned to Courtney.

"Um—are there any cliffs to walk off in this giant place?" Courtney had no idea what the answer could be. She was astonished when the others looked at each other in excitement. Her question had sparked an idea in each of them.

"The widow's walk!" they cried in unison, instantly taking off after Marc toward another part of the house.

What the hell's a widow's walk? Courtney wondered, suspecting she was about to find out.

She followed them to the third floor, part of which consisted of a lofty, open attic. Unfinished beams slanted away from the ceiling's highest point, where a flat, rectangular section of roof contained—to Courtney's surprise—a hinged trapdoor. A series of wooden steps led up to the hatch from the center of the room.

"Let's go!" said Marc, waving the others to follow as he mounted the stairs. Jenn, Zach, and Nate obeyed, with Courtney taking up the rear. She watched as he slid the latch to the side and lifted the door high enough to peek into the conference room beyond.

"The coast is clear," he said, turning back to look at the others. "It looks like everyone has finished up for the day."

Marc pushed open the hatch and climbed out onto the roof. Courtney and the others followed along behind.

The landscape that rose up before Courtney took her breath away. It was as if she'd emerged atop a mountain, a summit dwarfed only by the conference room's towering ceiling. She found the distance to the floor dizzying, and although the small rectangular area on which they stood was surrounded on all sides by fencing, the waist-high wooden structure appeared ancient and in significant need of repair.

Taking a deep breath to calm herself, she took a step back toward the center of the platform. There was no question that a fall from this height would be deadly. Turning slowly, she took in a full three-hundred-and-sixty-degree view of the conference room, instantly appreciating how small and insignificant the five teenagers had become.

"I don't see it," said Nate, his eyes searching the roof and railing.

Courtney had nearly forgotten the purpose of their mission—the doll! The platform on which they stood was barely large enough for the five of them and the hatch, and it was clear that the doll was not there. Had they been wrong in their interpretation of the riddle? Or . . .

Gathering her courage, Courtney stepped back to the ledge and peered over the railing at the shingled roof beyond. Marc had apparently had the same idea—he arrived at her side just a moment later.

"There it is!" he cried, pointing excitedly. That was when she saw it. The small cloth doll lay three-quarters of the way down the slanted surface. From a distance, it was difficult to see its facial features, but the brown hair was similar to Nate's, as were the blue jeans and short-sleeved red shirt it wore.

"I got it!" said Marc, throwing his leg over the railing.

"Be careful!" said Courtney as the others gathered around them.

"Marc—" said Nate.

"Don't worry, I got this—"

Misjudging the distance due to the roof's slant, Marc came down hard on the other side. He grabbed onto the railing to steady himself, and to everyone's horror, the ancient wood responded with a hideous *crack*.

The boy's eyes widened. He stood still for a moment, steadying himself, not even daring to breathe.

"Oops," he said at last, his face lighting up with a grin. "Close call—"

And that was when the slate shingle he was standing on gave way. Tearing free from its anchor point, it slid out from under his foot, pitching Marc forward and sending the full force of his body crashing into the old railing.

Courtney watched as the shingle slid down the roof, the stone-on-stone scraping sound like nails on a chalkboard. It struck the Nate-doll, pushing it to the side, before tumbling over the edge and plummeting out of sight.

As Marc fell into the dilapidated barrier, it crumpled beneath his weight, sending him sprawling onto the stone-covered surface of the roof. Holding onto the remains of the railing, he struggled to gain traction, but the sharp angle and the smooth, unstable condition of the shingles prevented his sneakers from gaining purchase. Suddenly, the dry, brittle section of wood in his grasp splintered away, and Marc began to slide . . .

"Marc!" cried Courtney as she threw out her hand, grasping at empty air. Marc reached for her, awkwardly grabbing her wrist—but his momentum yanked her forward, and Courtney began sliding face-first down the decline after him.

So, this is how it ends, she thought, her heart racing as she glided toward painful, disfiguring oblivion. *A tiny well-dressed stain on the library carpet. I never even graduated high school . . . I—*

"I've got you, Courtney!" cried Nate.

Strong hands clamped down on her ankles, stopping her forward movement and silencing the horrific scream that was coming from her own mouth. Several other shingles and railing pieces slid past her toward the edge.

"Marc—the doll!" she cried.

The boy, still grasping her tightly, saw the debris sliding past. Quickly locating his brother's effigy, he stretched out a leg and pressed his foot down on top of it. The avalanche of wreckage bounced off his shoe and tumbled harmlessly past, disappearing over the edge.

Thank God! thought Courtney, breathing a sigh of relief. *Nate's doll is safe—now all we need to do is get off this horrible roof, add the other dolls to their nooses, and we're out of here!*

"Oh, holy hell," said Zach.

"Don't move!" cried Jenn, clearly alarmed.

Damn, what now? Courtney thought, exhaustion setting in, the cold hard roofing tile beneath her cheek.

Ahemm.

It was the sound of a woman clearing her throat. Courtney, still on her stomach and suspended precariously between Nate and Marc, lifted her head to see what could have distressed the others—and instantly she understood. It was something out of a horror film. *Attack of the Thousand-Foot Librarian*, she would have called it.

Ms. Emily Brooks, school librarian, was heading directly for them, a stack of clipboards clutched in her arms. The towering behemoth of a woman looked as though she could have taken on both King Kong *and* Godzilla—and she was coming their way.

As luck would have it, in that moment, Courtney developed the most pressing, uncontrollable urge to sneeze.

"You've got to be kidding," she whimpered to herself. And then it happened . . .

ACHOO!

Courtney did her best to muffle the sound with her one free hand but failed miserably.

To her horror, Ms. Brooks paused directly beside the dollhouse. The woman searched the room with her eyes. They were mere moments from being discovered. Courtney imagined the woman's reaction: Ms. Brooks brandishing one of the deadly clipboards she carried, screeching in terror as she bashed them to bloody bits like unwelcomed cockroaches.

What happened was very different.

"Gesundheit," the librarian said to no one in particular—and then she walked away.

An hour later . . .

"This will never happen to another person," said Nate, dropping a match onto the kerosene-soaked miniature mansion. Standing outside behind the library, the five students watched the cursed sample of Victorian architecture go up in flame. Fire danced up and down the front porch, and before long, smoke was billowing from the holes in the brick where windows used to be.

After escaping the roof, Courtney, Marc, and the others had hurried through the house to the living room and placed the remaining three dolls into their nooses. Each one had dropped with a satisfying *ding* that echoed through the house. The chimes were followed by a single answering *dong*, and after a moment of disorienting nothingness, they were back in the conference room, once again in scale with their surroundings.

"Will Aunt Celia be able to find out where this thing came from?" asked Marc, poking at the now-crumbling structure with a stick. The blaze had already begun to die out.

"I don't know," replied Nate. "But she agreed it needed to be destroyed as soon as possible."

Courtney had remained mostly silent since they'd left the library. She wasn't sure how to react to their kindness. Marc and the others had treated her with respect and dignity. They'd valued her input and had even treated her as a friend.

"Courtney," said Nate, suddenly beside her. She met his eyes. "I wanted to thank you for all your help—and for saving my brother's life. That took courage, jumping after him on the roof."

"I—er—well, you saved *both* of us . . ." she replied.

"Still, thank you."

To Courtney's amazement, Nate leaned toward her and pulled her into a gentle hug.

"*Hey*, I want some," cried Marc, running over and wrapping his arms around them both. Before she knew it, Jenn and even Zach were there as well.

"Group squeeze," said Zach as he and Jenn joined in.

They're wrinkling my outfit. Courtney sighed.

The embrace lasted but a moment, yet to the lonely and misunderstood cheerleader, it meant everything in the world.

JENN: PART III

"This morning, I declared war on the white owl," said Jenn as she followed Aunt Celia down the dusty wooden stairs to the mansion's basement. Nate and his girlfriend, Alex, were a couple of steps behind. "But then it occurred to me—what can I really do? Spray it with a hose?"

At the bottom of the stairs, Aunt Celia reached up and pulled a string dangling in midair. A bare bulb blinked on, revealing a low, unfinished ceiling. Several antique chairs were now visible lining the nearby wall. On top of them sat a collection of small picture frames and other abandoned household items. The basement was the one part of the house that Jenn had never visited, and even now, most of it remained hidden in darkness.

Aunt Celia turned to Jenn as Nate and Alex joined them.

"You could have your parents call an exterminator," suggested Nate. He placed his hands on his hips. "They're used to dealing with all kinds of wild animals. They could probably capture it and take it away."

"And if that fails," added Alex, her face serious, "there are more . . . direct ways of dealing with it." She reached her hand into the air and when she pulled it back, Jenn saw that it contained the girl's magickal war quoit. Alex touched the circular flying weapon to her forearm, and it burst into flames. Nate's girlfriend, who happened to be the daughter of Malleus Hodge, was another witch with more experience than Jenn. Alex had been living with the Watsons since the battle at the cemetery.

"I appreciate the suggestions," replied Jenn. Her brows furrowed. "But I'm not ready to involve my parents, and I don't want to hurt the owl—at least not yet."

"It hasn't actually harmed you in any way, has it?" asked Aunt Celia. The concern was evident on her face. She stroked her chin with a forefinger as if considering something.

"No, it hasn't," said Jenn. "It just freaked me out a bit. The dead rabbit by the front door was more than I wanted first thing in the morning. It's probably nothing. With any luck, the owl will be gone by the time I get home."

Aunt Celia nodded. "You're probably right, but keep me informed. I'll do some research tonight. There might be something I can do to help."

Jenn smiled, returning the nod. She was glad to have Aunt Celia's support.

"Now, Nate," added Aunt Celia, "show me where you found the miniature replica of our home." She gestured toward the darkness ahead. Nate moved deeper into the basement, Aunt Celia following closely behind. Alex walked beside Jenn, her fiery weapon held high to help them see where they were going. Every so often, Nate stopped to yank the string of another light before going further into the gloom.

"Aunt Celia said you were interested in studying magick?" Alex asked, just loud enough for Jenn to hear.

Jenn looked at her and nodded. "Yes," she said. "There's so much that I need to learn about—spells, potions, familiars. I know next to nothing about being a witch."

"I can't say I know a whole lot myself," replied Alex. The revelation surprised Jenn. "I mean, there are certain things I can do very well. Other things I know very little about. My father always handled most of that stuff. To be honest, I never cared to learn. And the whole familiar thing—all I can say is: *hell no*, for me, that's never gonna happen!"

Jenn smiled at her. "You obviously feel strongly about that."

Alex shook her head, her red hair moving about her shoulders. The fire from her weapon illuminated the grimace on her face. "Be glad that you never had to spend time with my father's familiar—the horrible little beast was a nightmare in every sense of the word."

Jenn remembered seeing the leathery, winged imp for the first time at the church, when it stole the ancient spell book they were using to banish Hodge, the same book that she and Aunt Celia were attempting to reassemble.

"After living with it, I vowed never to take on a familiar of my own. Ugh—do I have stories! Later, if you're interested, I'll tell you about a particularly horrible experience I had in Boston."

"I'd love to hear it," replied Jenn. She smiled, enjoying the new connection she was making with Alex. She looked forward to getting to know the girl better.

As they traveled deeper into the old cellar, Jenn passed more abandoned furniture, building materials, and other random items left behind to gather dust. Cobwebs hung from the rafters in growing numbers, husks of desiccated insects decorating them like old, dead Christmas lights. Eventually, Nate stopped and pointed to a dark area where an archway was barely visible through the murk.

"I found it through there," he said. "Unfortunately, there are no more overhead lights." Nate pulled out his phone and shined its flashlight down a short corridor filled with junk, dust, and debris.

Aunt Celia stepped forward and peered through the opening. "I don't think I've ever been through there. Show me exactly where it was." Nate nodded and moved forward. He walked through the arch, his light bouncing around the dusty cement floor before him. The others followed him inside. Jenn saw footprints on the ground, evidence of Nate and Marc's earlier visit.

"What were you doing down in this dark, filthy space?" asked Alex. Her burning circlet revealed the confused expression she wore. She waved the weapon at a nearby collection of cobwebs. They burned away into nothingness.

"Just exploring," he replied, glancing back at them. "This place has so many interesting nooks and crannies. You never know what you might find."

Jenn skidded the edge of her sneaker across a section of floor, disturbing a thick patch of grime. "This place is pretty dusty," she said. "It must have taken a while to clean up the replica of the mansion if this is where it was stored."

Nate paused and turned around. Jenn saw the surprised look on his face. "You know, now that you mention it—the miniature house was surprisingly dust free. I really didn't have to clean it up at all. That's really strange." He turned back and pointed to a spot on the floor. "This is where I found it."

"Right here?" asked Aunt Celia, stepping forward. Nate nodded. "Can I borrow your phone for a second?" she added.

"Sure," said Nate, handing his aunt the cell. Aunt Celia bent down, shining its light across the ground. Jenn saw the rectangular section of floor where the miniature mansion had rested. It was dusty, but disturbed—as if something had been set down on top of the dust patch and later removed. She studied the narrow corridor, noting the junk and debris that lined the walls. At the very end of the corridor, Jenn noticed a filthy tapestry draped across a section of wall. Placing her hands on Nate's shoulders, she passed behind him, her back grazing the nearest wall. He glanced at her before returning his gaze to Aunt Celia's inspection.

Now at the dark end of the corridor, Jenn pulled out her phone, turning on the flashlight. She ran her hand across the tapestry. It was soft to the touch, and Jenn quickly realized that it was more likely an old blanket or quilt. It smelled musty. Jenn lifted an edge, dislodging a layer of dust that caught her by surprise, causing her to sneeze.

"Did you find something, Jenn?" asked Alex, suddenly at her side, her fiery circlet casting additional light on the old fabric.

"I'm not sure—" began Jenn. Before she could finish her sentence, however, the entire wall of cloth tumbled free, dislodging a cloud of dank-smelling debris. But that wasn't the worst of it. Jenn was shocked to see two shadowy figures looking back at her. They stood less than an arm's length away. Others could be seen behind them, moving quickly in their direction.

"Holy shit!" exclaimed Alex, jumping back. Surprisingly, one of the figures in front of them did the same. And that was when Jenn realized that they were looking at their own reflection. The figure that moved in sync with Alex was also holding a burning circlet in its hand.

"Oh my god," said Jenn, placing a hand on her forehead. "I nearly had a heart attack." She laughed nervously as Aunt Celia and Nate joined them.

"A giant mirror!" said Nate. "I didn't notice that the last time I was here. It takes up most of the wall!"

"Oh dear," said Aunt Celia. She had a troubled look on her face. The expression surprised Jenn.

"What is it?" Jenn asked. "Is something wrong?"

Aunt Celia pointed to the old quilt. "Help me cover it back up, will you?" With Jenn's, Alex's, and Nate's help, Aunt Celia draped the cloth over the oversized mirror. "Thanks, everyone," she said. "Now, let's head back upstairs. There are some things I must do."

As Aunt Celia turned to leave, Nate, Alex, and Jenn exchanged glances. *What just happened?* Jenn wondered. Nate shrugged his shoulders, turned, and hurried after Aunt Celia.

"I think she'll keep us wondering for a while," said Alex with a smirk.

Jenn nodded. "I think you're right. Shall we?" Jenn gestured toward Nate's disappearing back. It wasn't the first time Aunt Celia had dashed off to pursue some urgent matter without first filling them in. Jenn wondered what it was about the old mirror that had caused Aunt Celia concern.

Alex and Jenn moved back through the basement, switching off light bulbs as they went.

"Hey," said Alex, "how 'bout I tell you that story?"

"Sure, sounds like a plan!" exclaimed Jenn.

The two girls hurried up the steps and through the basement door. Jenn didn't for a moment regret leaving the dusty, dank darkness behind.

The Witchfinder's Familiar

Boston, Massachusetts Bay Colony, October 1691

"What's wrong with it?" asked Alex as she studied the whimpering creature on the floor in front of her. It rested on a large silk pillow, its leathery wings wrapped about its body like an infant's swaddling blanket. Its head remained uncovered, its face oddly human, its eyes closed. Perspiration glistened on its forehead between two stubby demonic horns, and sparse strands of hair lay matted to its scalp.

"*It* has a name," said her father with a hint of irritation. Still dressed in his night clothing, he stooped to look closer at the beast. Alex rolled her eyes.

"A name no one can pronounce," she mumbled under her breath. *Pix-el-fid-di-flex-ip.* She sounded out the syllables in her mind. *Try saying that three times fast.*

As her father's examination of the creature continued, Alex paced. She wasn't fond of her father's familiar, but its condition made her uncomfortable. In the eight years since its arrival, Alex had never once seen it fall ill. She glanced about the lofty rectangular room in which they'd been staying for the last several weeks. "Widow Murphy's guest cottage," her father had called it. The far end stood in shadows. This portion, however, was brightly lit and featured a pair of intricately carved oaken beds with tall canopies lined with rich, heavy draperies. The floor was covered in an alternating pattern of black and white marble tiles. Waist-high wainscoting lined the walls beneath red flower-swirled wallpaper. Alex nodded in approval at the assortment of colorful framed paintings, exquisite in every detail, that complimented the elaborate woodwork.

Returning her attention to her father and the beast, she lifted her long skirts and settled into one of the antique chairs that sat on either side of the small table where they ate their meals. From her position, she watched her father's inspection of the creature.

"I just don't understand it." He probed the imp's leathery wing-wrapped body with his fingers, and its moaning grew louder. The sound made Alex shudder.

"What's that?" she asked, pointing to a large, painful-looking lump on the beast's cheek. It was red and swollen, an angry welt marring the skin. "It looks like it was hit by something. Or maybe stung." She'd seen plenty of bees out here in the countryside. A sudden thought struck her, and her eyes grew wide. "You don't think its catching, do you? An illness, like the pox, or the plague?"

"I don't know, Alexandra." Her father shook his head. "But whatever it is—"

A sudden flurry of feathers appeared on the table beside Alex. The ruffled white hen strutted forward, its neck lurching with each step, its claws scratching grooves into the shiny wooden surface. At the edge of the table, it bent down, its beak closing about a lone ant which it swallowed with a shake of its head.

"Ewww—" cried Alex in disgust as she jumped to her feet.

"Alexandra!" said her father sharply, his face showing anger. "I told you to keep those things under control!"

She grabbed the chicken between two hands, tossing it to the floor. "I don't know what you expect me to do," she replied, wiping her hands on her skirts. "They keep getting back in. Call it what you will, but we *are* living in a—"

"Alexandra—" began her father, his temper rising.

"Maaaaa," came the cry of another animal. This time, a brown-and-white goat appeared, emerging from the room's darkened end, its hooves clacking on the decorative stone tile. Her father's face twisted into a frown.

"You can't blame them," snapped Alex, matching her father's expression. "They're hungry. We were supposed to feed them half an hour ago. If we don't get to the chores soon, Widow Murphy will—"

A loud knocking came from the other end of the room. Her father's eyes traveled from the imp to Alex as the color drained from his face. "God's blood! It's that dreadful woman," he said, his concern for the imp forgotten for the moment. "Alexandra, do something!" He made a wide sweeping gesture before motioning toward his own rumpled sleeping attire.

It irritated Alex that although her father was a powerful warlock, he relied constantly on *her* magick. With a sigh, she closed her eyes and let the magick course through her. When she opened them, the room's elegant features were already dissolving. The fancy woodwork and art melted from the walls, leaving wide, unfinished planks in their place. The elaborate canopy beds vanished, revealing the rough piles of straw on which she and her father had been forced to sleep. And as she dismissed the rest of the impressive glamour that masked their unimpressive living quarters, the banging intensified. Light now filtered through the gaps in the building's rough exterior, illuminating the barn door at the far end of the two-story structure, its surface shaking with every blow.

"Goodman Hodgins!" commanded Widow Murphy, her voice like fingernails dragged across slate. "I insist that you open this door at once!"

Alex's father met her gaze before pointing hurriedly at the hell beast, still resting in the middle of the room, now on a pile of straw. Without another word, he turned and hurried across the hay-strewn floor toward the door and the woman waiting on the other side.

Again, Alex called upon her magick, and the imp, fortunately silent for the moment, faded from view. Her father passed the small pens that contained the farm animals they'd been hired to care for. He plucked his tall, brimmed hat from a nail by the door, placing it on his head. Before he could raise the heavy wooden beam that barred entry to the barn, she used her magick to mask his worn night clothing. A long-sleeved, button-down jacket with thick cuffs appeared over a pair of baggy shorts, cinched at the knees. On his calves were dark socks that disappeared into high-tongued leather shoes. Her father glanced down at his newly altered vestments and, apparently satisfied, threw open the barn door, letting in the morning sun.

"Goodwife Murphy," he said, bowing to the grim-faced older woman standing outside. "How truly lovely to see you."

The widow's features softened only slightly at her father's show of deference. "Save your insincere pleasantries," she said. "We have business to attend to, and you know I hate being kept waiting."

"And so, we shall leave at once," said Widow Murphy, her face serious, a trace of condescension in her voice. The woman wore a dark cloak to ward off the brisk morning air. Her white silk bonnet was trimmed in gold lace, a quiet reminder of both her wealth and status within the community.

"My dear lady, I'm afraid that is quite impossible—" began Alex's father. Alex stood behind him as he spoke through the open barn door. The older woman's expression told Alex that there was no room for negotiation. Her father apparently felt differently. "I can't possibly pick up and leave on such short notice."

"Nonsense! You were hired to perform the tasks I assign to you, and this is what I require." Her brows knit together. "If you would prefer to find work—and lodgings—elsewhere, then you are free to do so . . ."

"But we haven't yet fed the livestock," said her father. "And what of the other tasks planned for today?"

"Surely on this one occasion, the girl can handle the daily chores on her own," she said. "My brother, Jonathan, already has the wagon ready to take us to Dorchester. The colder weather will shortly be upon us. I've offered him your services to help finish the repairs on his barn. It should take no more than a day or two, but as I said, time is of the essence."

"And you will . . . be going along as well?" her father asked. He frowned, his brows furrowing as he adjusted the brim of his capotain hat.

"Certainly," she replied with a nod. "It's been a while since I've visited my brother's family. They're thrilled that I've agreed to visit."

I'll bet, thought Alex, unable to suppress a grin. It occurred to her that if both her father and the widow left for a time, most of her day-to-day stress would go with them.

"Well, surely we can't both go," her father said hurriedly. "Who would inspect my daughter's work?" He shook his head. "No. I must insist that one of us remain behind to ensure that everything is completed to your exacting standards." Her father turned to Alex, and their eyes locked.

What are you doing? Alex glared icicles at him. He looked away.

"You do have a point there," said the widow with a tilt of the head. As the woman paused to consider her father's words, a wave of anxiety washed over Alex. The last thing she wanted was to be stranded alone with Goodwife Murphy, at her beck and call. How could her father suggest such a thing?

"Not to worry, Mother," said a new voice that Alex recognized immediately. "I'll stay behind to supervise." It was Rebecca, the widow's daughter. She was close to Alex in age and every bit as insufferable as her mother. Alex's attempts to befriend the girl had failed. Rebecca considered Alex her inferior, and she went to great lengths to make that clear to anyone who would listen.

"Are you sure, my dear?" the widow asked, turning to the young woman as she approached. "I know how much you were looking forward to accompanying us." She rested her hand on Rebecca's shoulder. Dark locks escaped Rebecca's bonnet, contrasting her alabaster skin.

"It's okay. Truly. I'm always happy to help," the girl replied with a smile. Her gaze landed on Alex, and as their eyes met, Rebecca's grin took on new meaning. "No need to worry, Mother," she said. "Alexandra and I will have a *wonderful* time together."

"But you can't leave me here with Rebecca," said Alex as her father closed and barred the barn door. "She hates me—she'll do everything she can to make me miserable." Alex let her remaining glamours dissipate, leaving her father once again in his night clothes. The imp reappeared, dozing on the floor. It began to shake as if having a seizure. After a moment, the tremors stopped.

"Alexandra, there's nothing to be done about it," her father replied, his attention on the imp. He knelt beside the creature and placed a hand on its forehead before glancing up and meeting her gaze. "Besides, *I* received the prickly end of that stick. Not only will I be subjected to the hard labors of barn repair, but I'll have to endure her bothersome company to Dorchester and back!" He gestured toward Alex's arm and grimaced. "Can't you do something about that?"

Alex looked down to see the stream of blood dripping from the gash in her forearm. Her magick was blood magick, and for it to work, blood had to flow. With a quick thought, she masked the wound with an illusion of fresh pink skin. "Neither of us like it here. Surely there are other jobs. Why don't we just leave?" Alex placed her hands on her hips, her expression pleading. "We could go somewhere else. Somewhere where the people are nicer."

"Alex, we've already invested valuable time here, getting to know the widow and her neighbors. And I've made the acquaintances of several of Boston's leaders. You know why we're here. You know what we've been working toward. If there is a witch in this town, one woman that the villagers will believe is under the influence of Satan, it's the widow Murphy. This is my opportunity to demonstrate my value to the community by exposing her and the dangers she represents."

"But we have no reason to believe that she's a witch," said Alex.

"It's not important for us to believe it," said her father with a frown. "It's only important that the townsfolk believe it. And they will. The widow has offended many with her overbearing demeanor."

Alex simply nodded. She didn't agree with her father's plan, but she'd long since learned that once he'd made his mind up, there was no dissuading him. The fact that they were witches, hunting others who likely were not, seemed hypocritical to her, but there was little she could do about it.

Out of the corner of her eye, she caught the flutter of wings. It was another chicken, forcing its way into the barn through a gap in the planks. *It's probably hungry,* she thought. With a sigh, she turned to fetch a pail of feed.

"Oh, and Alexandra?" her father called after her. She spun to find him moving about, collecting items for the upcoming journey. He gestured to the imp. "Obviously I can't take him with me. You'll have to keep an eye on him while I'm away."

"I'll have to *what*?" she asked in disbelief. Before her father could respond, the hell beast lurched awake, sat upright, and began to wail. The expression of agony on its face caused Alex's stomach to tighten. She dropped the pail of feed, and it landed on its side, spilling its contents. She covered both ears with her hands.

This day just keeps getting better and better, she thought.

Later that day, after Alex had gathered the morning's eggs, fed and watered the animals, milked the two Shorthorn cows, mucked the horse stalls, and pumped, hauled, and heated five buckets of water for Rebecca's afternoon bath, she left the widow's kitchen with an armload of apple preserves for the root cellar beneath the barn. Once outside, she glanced at the sky, noting dark clouds to the west. There was a fresh chill in the air, and Alex suspected that a storm was on its way.

Gently hefting the glass containers, Alex approached the barn door. She nudged a chicken out of the way with her foot and slipped inside. When Alex reached the small dining table, she placed all five jars on top of its scratched, slightly wobbly surface. She yanked the strings of her bonnet, letting her hair tumble free. Almost as an afterthought, she pulled two fresh apples from the pockets of her skirts and placed them beside the preserves. Alex had "borrowed" them from the widow's kitchen when Rebecca wasn't looking.

Call it payment for dealing with Rebecca all day, she thought, a playful smirk blossoming across her face. The widow's daughter had followed Alex from chore to chore, instructing her on the proper methods for completing each task. Alex was sure the girl had never performed any of them herself.

Alex made her way to the barn's north wall. She bent down and brushed away a patch of loose straw to reveal a large metal ring embedded in the floor. Grasping the loop, she stood, tugging firmly, until a square section of wood rose into the air. Hay tumbled from its edges as she pulled and then pushed the trap door to its fully open position. Although she'd been aware of the hatch, she'd never had the occasion to look inside. The end of a ladder descended into the dark root cellar below, but not much more was visible. Walking back to the table, she picked up two of the preserve jars and slid them carefully into her skirt pockets.

Quickly, Alex glanced around the room. She was relieved to see that her father's familiar was still snoring soundly in one corner. Before leaving that morning, she'd hastily tossed an old quilt on top of it to hide it from prying eyes. Both the imp and the quilt were just as she had left them.

Alex used a fingernail to reopen the most recent cut on her forearm. As the blood and magick began to flow, a ball of light appeared inside the root cellar, and when she returned to the opening, this time she could see everything inside. The hole was six feet square, the dirt walls insulated with bundles of straw. Two of the walls were lined with shelves that contained an assortment of canning jars, all lined up in neat, even rows.

Carefully, she climbed down the wooden ladder and removed the containers from her pockets. She studied the older canned items, finding there everything from pickled eggs to peaches, corn to pears. A layer of dust coated everything. She placed the apple preserves on an empty shelf, and as she pulled her hand away, a loud crash from above caused her to jump.

What in the world? Alex's heart began to race. Immediately she thought of the imp. Had it woken up? Grasping the rungs tightly, she scrambled out of the cellar, somehow certain that she'd find the creature staggering about the barn in its fevered delirium.

What she found was quite different. The brown-and-white goat stood by the table, chomping on one of her fresh apples, the shattered remains of three jars of preserves oozing between its feet. The animal had, once again, escaped from its pen.

God, help me, thought Alex, feeling relieved at the sight of the goat. The thought of dealing with the imp had filled her with anxiety. She knew little about the creature or what ailed it. How could she ever care for it? If she were lucky, the beast would remain asleep until her father returned.

Alex grabbed the goat by the scruff of the neck and guided it back to its pen. With a gentle shove, she pushed it inside, swinging the gate closed behind it. A shovel rested against a nearby wall. She grabbed it and returned to the table to clean up the preserves. Before she picked up the first piece of glass, however, the imp began to screech.

It was the same agonizing wail she'd heard that morning, and it filled her with dread. She turned to see the creature stumbling about, the old quilt still draped over its head. It crashed into the side of the barn and toppled to the floor, its cries growing even louder.

Near panic, Alex rushed to the barn door and barred it with the heavy wooden crossbeam. If the keening continued, she knew, it was only a matter of time before Rebecca showed up, and Rebecca was the last person she wanted to deal with at that moment.

Alex ran past the table, her shoes crunching broken glass. When she reached the hell beast, it was already regaining its feet. She clamped her hands over her ears to ward off its piercing cries, and as she did so, she noticed that an orange glow had begun radiating from beneath the quilt. Before her eyes, the fabric began to smolder. It burned away from the inside as the imp's body erupted in flames. Alex had seen the imp use its hellfire in the past—she knew no harm would come to the creature, but in a wooden barn filled with dry hay, fire meant only one thing—disaster.

The beast swayed unsteadily, staring past Alex as if she weren't there. Somehow, she had to wake it from its stupor. "Pix!" she cried, trying to get it to acknowledge her. "Pixelfidiflexip!" Its name felt strange upon her lips.

The blazing creature's head swiveled, its eyes locking onto her. She saw no recognition on its face. Fire danced across its forehead, illuminating its two stubby horns. Her eyes were drawn to the welt on its cheek. Alex gasped. Incredibly, it seemed to have tripled in size! The beast lurched toward her, its flaming wings unfurling. Its high-pitched screams rang in her ears as it picked up speed.

Alex dove to the side as it rushed past her and took to the air. She stared in disbelief as the imp soared unsteadily above her, its wings struggling to keep it airborne. A small fire flared at her feet, and she paused to stomp it out before it could spread. There, in the straw beside the scorch marks, she noticed her remaining apple, the one left uneaten by the goat.

A blast of air blew past Alex, violently tossing her hair. She looked up to see the imp rising higher into the rafters. She was relieved to see that its flames had subsided, perhaps tamped down by the heavy flapping of its wings. Its erratic flight path took it the full length of the barn, and just moments before Alex thought it would crash into the wall above the door, it turned back toward her, narrowly missing the slant of the roof.

The imp dove at her. Whether it was intentional or not, Alex couldn't tell. She crouched down, and at the last second, the imp shot skyward once again. With a splintering crash, it struck a rafter and was tossed sideways into another. The imp tumbled through the air like a goose shot out of the sky. It landed high above her in the nearby hayloft where it fell still, its screeching silenced.

From her vantage point, Alex couldn't see the creature's body. A narrow ladder led up to the loft, but its wooden rungs appeared worn and unsteady, and she had no wish to attempt them alone. She looked down at her hands. They were trembling.

"Alexandra!" cried an angry, excited voice. "Open up!" The barn door rattled against the crossbeam that held it closed as Rebecca tried to push her way inside.

Oh God, thought Alex, her heart racing. *Not Rebecca. Not now.* Her worst fears were coming true.

And that was when the imp, for the third time that day, began to screech.

"Alexandra?" shouted Rebecca, her voice barely audible over the hell beast's howl. "What are you doing? Open up this minute!" The barn door continued to rattle against its restraint.

In full panic mode, Alex's eyes searched the room for something that could help her. She found nothing. There wasn't even a secondary exit out of the barn. She had no idea what to do. The creature's screaming had set her nerves on fire, short-circuiting her ability to think. She looked back at the loft to find the imp now standing unsteadily at its edge.

"Pix!" she yelled, trying once again to get its attention. The beast failed to respond. Her eyes fell on the apple lying at her feet. She bent down, picked it up, and threw it at the imp with all her might.

To her surprise, relief, and horror, the apple struck the imp squarely in the forehead. Instantly the beast's cries stopped as it lost consciousness. Its knees buckled, and its body tumbled forward over the edge of the loft. Alex watched in awe as, seemingly in slow motion, the creature plummeted headfirst toward the floor.

With a mind-numbing *crack*, its skull struck the straw-covered dirt, the momentum carrying its body forward. It landed limply on its back, its leathery wings outstretched at its sides, its neck twisted at an unnatural angle.

Oh my God! she thought. A sense of dread washed over her as she stared at the motionless creature. *I killed my father's familiar! He'll never forgive me!*

"Alex!" Rebecca had begun pounding on the door again. Her heart still thumping in her chest, Alex masked the imp with her magick. Its broken corpse vanished from sight.

She turned and ran to the door. With some effort, she lifted the crossbeam and let it fall to the floor. She pulled the door inward several inches until she could see Rebecca through the opening. The sky had continued to darken. It looked like the heavens could release torrents of rain at any moment. The girl was wrapped from neck to ankle in a quilt, her feet bare despite the cool weather, her hair still dripping from her bath. Their eyes met.

"Alex!" cried Rebecca, the anger evident on her face. "Tell me at once what is going on in there." Her forehead wrinkled. "Are you killing a pig?"

"Er, yeah," Alex replied quickly, her mind a jumble. "Uh, I mean, no. Of course not . . . say, can you come back later?" She winced inside, knowing how bad she sounded.

"No! I cannot come back later!" Rebecca cried. "What was that hideous noise? Let me in at once!" She shoved the door with both hands, but it sprung back when it met Alex's foot. "Al-l-l-lex!" The girl was getting angrier by the second.

"*I* made that sound," said Alex, grasping for any remotely believable response. She placed a hand on the doorframe. "It was me. I was, uh . . ." She was unable to finish the sentence. What could she possibly say that Rebecca would accept?

"Don't lie to me. I know you're up to something. I—" Rebecca's mouth fell open, and her eyes went wide. "What happened to your arm?"

Alex followed Rebecca's gaze, horrified to see the fresh blood dribbling from the gash in her forearm. In her panic, she had forgotten to mask it. "I broke a jar of preserves," said Alex, thinking quickly. "I cut myself on it. It hurt, and I screamed. Listen—I really have to go now." Without another word, Alex slammed the barn door closed and leaned all of her weight against it. If she were lucky, Rebecca would take the hint and leave. Realistically, she knew that was not about to happen. It would take much more than a closed door to get Rebecca off her back.

As if in answer to her prayers, a crash of thunder shook the building, followed by the sounds of rain. Torrents and torrents of rain. The rushing downpour soothed her nerves. Alex knew that Rebecca would never endure such a soaking if she had a choice in the matter. Alex spun and reopened the door far enough to peek outside. A streak of lightning brightened the sky, and in the distance, she saw Rebecca fleeing toward the house as fast as her legs could carry her.

With a sigh of relief, Alex shut the door. Hefting the wooden beam, she slid it carefully back into place, securing her privacy for the moment. She knew that Rebecca would be back in the morning, if not sooner, but for the time being, at least she'd be able to settle her nerves and plan for their next encounter.

Exhausted both mentally and physically, Alex walked slowly past the animal pens. The goat was nibbling at something on the floor, and its head popped up at her approach. The pigs rested on piles of hay, seemingly unphased by the recent commotion or the onset of the storm. A stray hen strutted about an empty stall looking for insects, its cohorts likely sheltered in the coop outside.

When she reached the opposite end of the barn, she dismissed the illusion that masked the imp's twisted body. It lay where it fell, its bat-like wings splayed out to the sides. Her father entrusted it to her care, and now the creature was dead. How would she break the news to him? How would he react to her failure?

She picked up the shovel she'd left by the table. For now, she would bury the imp's body in straw to minimize the chance of it being seen. A more permanent solution would have to wait for her father's return. She approached the hell beast and bent to examine it.

Instantly, Alex recoiled in horror.

The swollen welt on the creature's cheek had grown even larger—but that wasn't all. Still angry and inflamed, it appeared engorged with fluid, a bloated sack of skin pulled taught by its unimaginable contents.

Other nightmarish cysts hung from other parts of its body—its neck, chest, groin, and thighs. Each of them as bulging and grotesque as the one on its face. Alex's stomach began to churn. Gently, she nudged one of the distended pouches with the edge of the shovel. It jiggled slightly and then burst, spewing its blood-streaked, pus-filled contents. The stench that accompanied it took her breath away. Alex saw what appeared to be fragments of bone poking out from the ruptured flesh.

Oh God, Alex thought. *You must really hate me.*

She clamped her hand over her mouth and ran, the shovel falling to the floor. When she reached the door, she shoved the crossbar to the side with all her might and slipped outside. Lightning streaked the sky as the rain fell in torrents. Muddy puddles soaked the hems of Alex's skirts, but she didn't care. With her face held high, she stood there for some time and let the storm wash away all the grime, sweat, and stress of the last twelve hours.

Alex woke to the sensation of something wriggly and wet being dragged across her face. She bolted upright and opened her eyes. She was startled to see a set of eyes staring back at her.

"Leave me alone," she groaned, pushing the goat away with an elbow. The goat bleated and wandered off. Alex flopped back onto the straw.

All night she'd dreamed of the imp tumbling from the loft to its death. Part of her couldn't wait for her father to return to relieve her of the burden his absence had placed upon her. The other part was terrified—terrified of his reaction to the imp's death, of his disappointment in her handling of the situation, and of the punishment she was certain to receive.

Alex rose, running her fingers through her hair to remove the hay that had stuck to it overnight. She usually slept in a bonnet to minimize the need for grooming, but last night after the rain shower, she'd simply reentered the barn, barred the door, shrugged off her wet clothing, and collapsed into bed. She looked around the barn, noting all the things left undone. The broken canning jars still littered the floor. While some remnants of drying preserves remained, much of it was gone, eaten, she assumed, by the goat. It stood nearby, licking at some of the offending apple residue.

The hatch to the root cellar was wide open, a lone chicken pecking at the dirt beside its wooden frame. And not far from that was the limp form of the imp. She avoided looking directly at it. Her stomach lurched when she thought of the horrible sacks of fluid covering the beast's body. *God, don't let it be catching,* she prayed silently. She knew she had to deal with the creature immediately. Rebecca could show up at any moment, and the girl could not be allowed to see it. But first, Alex had to get dressed.

As she pulled on her clothing, it occurred to her that she had no idea of the time. Although it was bright outside, the early morning rays that normally filtered in through the barn's walls were absent. *How long did I sleep?* she wondered. Her heart began to race as she realized it could be close to noon or possibly even later.

Alex hurried to the barn door and lifted the crossbar. Peering outside, her fears were confirmed. The sun was high overhead. Her day was off to a very late start. She was surprised that Rebecca hadn't already come looking for her. Most likely, the girl had gone into town for morning services, but even so, she should have been back by now. Perhaps Rebecca had stayed late to socialize with her friends—boorish, pretentious girls, all of them. Alex pushed the door closed and hefted the wooden beam back into its brackets. She had no time to waste. She had to hide the imp's body.

Alex hurried past the table, careful to avoid the shards of glass. She bent to retrieve the shovel she'd dropped on the floor beside the beast. For now, she'd push the corpse under the nearest pile of hay, and she and her father could deal with it later. With the shovel grasped in both hands, she turned her attention to the imp.

Alex gasped in surprise. Her mouth remained open, her eyes widening as she stared at the creature in front of her. Despite the fear and revulsion that threatened to overtake her, she leaned in for a closer look. Impossibly, the cysts were even larger than they'd been the prior afternoon. They were now the size of small cabbages, the surrounding skin stretched translucent by their putrid contents.

God, what is going on here? she wondered. Her stomach twisted at the sight before her. Surely, the lesions couldn't continue to grow. Could they?

To her horror, one of the fluid sacks shook. It was just a slight ripple, but that was all it took to send her blood pumping faster. She stared at it, daring it to move again, to prove that her stressed-out mind wasn't just playing tricks on her.

And that was when she saw it. Something shifted beneath the surface.

She fell backward, dropping the shovel, but her eyes remained fixed on the spot. A section of skin lifted, pushed upward by something firm—something shaped very much like a hand. Four small fingers became visible, pressing against skin that was already straining against its contents—grotesque digits with pointy-looking tips. *Claws?* Alex wondered.

She struggled backward as the horrible cyst burst open, spraying gobs of blood-streaked fluid in all directions. Although she managed to avoid the worst of the spatter, her skirts did not go unscathed. Instantly the putrid stench that she remembered from the day before assailed her nostrils, but she barely noticed. Her attention was fully focused on the damp ball of leathery flesh that had rolled free of the imp's corpse and was now rocking back and forth on the floor in front her.

A pair of bat-like wings separated from the moist mass and began to unfurl, revealing the very un-bat-like creature inside. It wobbled on short, unsteady legs as it rose to its full upright position, its round head seemingly large for its body. Although it stood no more than a foot in height, its appearance sent chills through Alex's body. Through the goo, she could make out its humanlike features and the tiny, pointed horns that sprouted from its forehead.

The creature was a perfect miniature duplicate of her father's imp.

"No way," Alex whimpered, both shocked and terrified. She regained her feet just as the beast, without warning, burst into flames. The fire went out almost instantly, but not before burning away the rancid fluid that coated its body. Alex stumbled backward, nearly tripping over the hen that had wandered into her path. The agitated bird released a squawk, changed direction, and scurried out of the way.

Immediately, the impling's attention turned to the fleeing hen. Its eyes bulging with excitement, the creature's mouth fell open to reveal tiny needlelike teeth dripping with saliva. It lurched forward on shaky legs, taking several quick steps before leaping into the air, its wings carrying it swiftly in pursuit of its feathered prey.

Alex cringed as the beast landed on top of the bird. The hen's screeching cries stopped abruptly as the impling tore into it. Tooth and claw shredded flesh and bone in an explosion of feathers.

Horrified and afraid that the impling would turn on her next, Alex grabbed the fallen shovel. She raised its metal end into the air as she moved quickly toward the creature. With all her strength, she brought the makeshift weapon down upon the small hell beast's head.

At the last instant, however, it leaped out of the way. Alex grunted as the shovel struck the bloody, mutilated chicken carcass left behind in its path. The impling took to the air, its wings lifting it high above Alex's head. She raised the shovel, her eyes following the creature as it flitted about the rafters, chittering wildly.

Suddenly, the impling dove directly at Alex. She ducked as it swooped past her, its claws barely missing her head. It snagged a lock of hair instead. She cried out in pain as a patch tore free, and her scalp began to bleed.

Alex's fear and revulsion turned to anger. The next time the creature dove at her, she swung at it with the shovel, this time making contact. The impling met the hard surface with a clang and was sent flying, its chittering silenced. It struck the wooden planks of the wall and dropped, crumpling to the floor. As it struggled to right itself, Alex ran at it, shovel readied for combat. Before she could reach it, however, the creature slipped through one of the gaps in the wallboards and was gone.

Alex wasn't sure what to do—should she go after it? The impling was flying free outside, and it could be anywhere. If she did find it, how would she catch it? She wished more than ever that her father would return. He'd know what to do.

Alex caught movement out of the corner of her eye. At first, she thought the impling had found another way back into the barn. When she realized what was happening, however, her legs grew weak, and her body began to tremble. The shovel tumbled from her grasp. Her vision blurred. She reached for the nearby table to steady herself, for a moment fearing she'd lose consciousness.

The dead imp's body was moving, the remaining fluid sacks jiggling, their tiny inhabitants struggling to break free. Alex had forgotten all about the others! In quick succession, each of the flesh bags burst open, spewing their horrible contents. One, two, three—four baby imps rolled free of the imp's body.

Alex watched, paralyzed, as their leathery wings began to uncurl and unfurl, revealing the small bodies beneath. The newborns rose slowly, shakily to their feet, their bodies dripping with goo. Just like before, each of them erupted in flames. The stench-ridden birthing fluids burned away quickly and then, one by one, each of their fires extinguished.

Oh God, I have to get out of here, thought Alex, gathering her nerve. She turned and ran for the barn door. Hearing their excited cries, she looked back to find all four sets of bulging eyes focused on her. Immediately the creatures began moving in pursuit.

At the door, Alex struggled to lift the heavy crossbeam. It rattled in its brackets but refused to pull free. Terrifying seconds passed as Alex wrestled with the bar, knowing that at any moment the flock of tiny demons would be upon her.

The cry of an animal reached her ears. Alex risked a glance over her shoulder. It was the goat. The frightened animal was running madly about the barn, the swarm of hell beasts close on its tail. The implings, finding closer prey, had stopped chasing her—for the moment at least.

One of the small beasts landed on the goat's back, its claws penetrating the animal's fur. With a screech, the goat's frantic pace picked up speed. It crashed into the old table, knocking it on its side. Running out of room, the animal slowed long enough to turn its body in a different direction. As it bolted toward the opposite wall, two more of the creatures landed on it. The goat hurled itself to the floor, rolling on its back in a desperate attempt to dislodge the hell beasts. It worked, but only briefly. All four creatures landed on the animal's exposed belly and began to eat.

Alex cringed but couldn't divert her eyes. The goat, writhing in agony, twisted about, trying unsuccessfully to regain its feet as the implings tore into its flesh. Its thrashing brought it too close to the open root cellar. With a despairing bleat, it tumbled over the edge and vanished from sight, taking all four hell beasts with it.

Seeing her opportunity, Alex ran to the trap door and yanked it closed. It swung shut with a heavy thud, sealing the ravenous creatures inside. She plopped down on top of it for a moment to catch her breath.

Oh my God, she thought as relief flooded through her. *I'm still alive.* The implings wouldn't be able to lift the heavy wooden hatch. She heard chittering and the occasional sound of smashing glass. She glanced at the body of her father's familiar. She despised the creature more than ever. Even in death, it had caused her so much trouble.

Alex rose and approached the barn door. Another shove loosened the heavy crossbeam. She lifted it, letting it fall to the ground. Stepping outside, she scanned the area for any trace of the missing impling. The sun was high in the sky. Patches of mud, left over from the previous night's storm, dotted the ground between the barn and the main house. The young hell beast was nowhere in sight. Alex stood there for several seconds, scanning the horizon, studying the trees, looking everywhere she could think of for the creature, to no avail.

Giving up, she turned back. Alex had left the barn a complete disaster. She needed to get it back in order quickly so that she could begin the daily chores.

"Alexandra!" called a voice.

God, please, not now, she thought. Alex turned to see Rebecca. The girl hurried toward her from the direction of the house, stepping carefully to avoid the patches of mud. Alex had been right. Rebecca was dressed in her finest morning service clothes.

"Alexandra," repeated Rebecca when she reached Alex, "we never finished our conversation yesterday."

"Good morning, Rebecca," said Alex, forcing herself to remain calm. After the day she'd been having, she was in no mood for the girl. "I'm very busy at the moment, and I don't have time to talk." She turned and started for the barn.

"Alexandra! You'll stop at once!" commanded Rebecca, her voice dripping with condescension.

Irritated, Alex turned back to Rebecca, preparing a witty retort. And that's when she saw the hell beast. It shot toward them through the air, its wings flapping, its eyes bulging, its mouth a toothy, open rictus. Rebecca remained oblivious to the creature approaching from behind.

Alex lurched forward, shoving Rebecca to the ground in the nick of time. The girl landed in the mud, and Alex landed on top of her, the impling missing them by mere inches.

"What are you doing?" shouted Rebecca, struggling to free herself. "Get off me. Are you insane?"

Alex held the girl down as the hell beast turned toward them for another pass. A desperate idea popped into her head. Using her magick, she created the perfect glamour of a hen and sent it scurrying off toward the chicken coop on the far side of the barn. To her relief, the impling took the bait and flew off in pursuit. She had doomed the other chickens, but with any luck, the creature would remain occupied until Alex could rid herself of Rebecca.

As soon as the creature was gone, Alex rolled off Rebecca and stood. Offering her a hand, she pulled the agitated girl to her feet.

"How dare you!" cried Rebecca. She was furious. Mud spattered her hair and clothing. "Just look at me! When my mother gets home—" Rebecca's eyes grew wide, her face contorting with rage. She lunged for Alex, and the two girls went down again in a muddy tangle of arms and legs.

Alex fought off the blows that rained down on her. She shoved Rebecca to the side, flipping the girl onto her back. Using her hands and the weight of her body, she sunk the girl's shoulders into the mud. Rebecca's legs thrashed, but with both arms pinned, there was little she could do to free herself.

"Why can't you just leave me alone?" asked Alex, staring into the girl's face.

"Because you," began Rebecca, her voice slow and full of hatred, "need to learn your place in this world."

The girl's haughty expression filled Alex with fury. She was tired of being judged. She was tired of not fitting in, and she was tired of other people telling her who she was supposed to be. Who did this girl think she was?

Releasing one of Rebecca's arms, Alex scooped up a handful of mud and smeared it all over Rebecca's shocked face.

"And you, Rebecca," said Alex, "need to learn how to be nice."

"Alexandra!" Dread filled Alex as she recognized her father's angry voice. She looked up to see him jumping down from the horse-drawn wagon. In all the commotion, she hadn't noticed its approach. An excited Widow Murphy descended from the far side of the wagon with the help of her brother, Jonathan.

"You horrible thing," the widow cried as she hurried toward them, her eyes locked upon Alex. "What have you done to my Rebecca?"

Alex's father reached them first. He bent down, grabbed hold of Alex's arm, and lifted her to her feet.

The widow arrived a moment later. "Jonathan, help Rebecca at once!" she commanded. Jonathan quickly obeyed.

"Alexandra," said her father angrily as he maintained his grip on her arm. "Tell me what's going on! What have you done?"

"I'll tell you what she's done," interjected Rebecca, once more on her feet. She wiped a blob of mud from her face. "That dimwitted creature attacked me for no reason!"

"Is that true, Alexandra?" asked her father. All three of the adults were staring at her.

"Well, not exactly," Alex replied, avoiding eye contact. There was no way she could tell them the real reason for her actions.

"My poor Rebecca," said the widow. "Come to me, my dear. Let's get you cleaned up."

"She attacked me, Mother," said Rebecca in the most timid, victimized voice Alex had ever heard her use.

"I know, dear. The girl is clearly uncivilized." The widow shot another glance toward Alex. Turning to Alex's father, she added, her voice raised: "We will address this matter after I've had a chance to freshen up. I suggest you speak with your daughter at once." She then turned to her brother. "Jonathan, please retrieve my trunk from the wagon and bring it into the house."

Jonathan grabbed the widow's luggage, and the three of them went inside.

As soon as they were gone, Alex's father spoke. "Alexandra, I'm very disappointed in you. What were you thinking?" He dragged her forcefully toward the open barn door.

"But you don't understand," she said. "The imp—" She suddenly found herself at a loss for words. Where to even begin?

Suddenly, an agitated chittering sound could be heard from inside. Had one of the implings freed itself? Had the escaped impling returned?

"What about the imp?" her father asked. "It sounds like he's feeling better, at least. Weren't you able to keep him quiet?"

Her father thought it was his familiar making those sounds—but his familiar was dead. The moment they entered the barn, her father would see its corpse. Alex had to break the news to him right away.

"Father, wait. I have to tell you something," she began as her father pushed her through the door. "I'm sorry to tell you this, but the imp . . . it's—"

Alex's mouth dropped open. She couldn't believe her eyes. There, scratching frantically at the root cellar's hatch, was her father's imp, and it was very much alive. It turned its head briefly toward them before returning to its frenzied clawing.

"The imp is what, Alexandra?" said her father. His eyes traveled around the barn, falling upon the overturned table, the broken preserve jars, and the chicken carcass before returning to the distressed hell beast. "What on earth happened here? And why is Pix so interested in the root cellar?" Freeing Alex's arm, her father hurried to the trap door. To Alex's horror, he bent down and grasped the metal ring. He began to lift it.

"Father, no!" cried Alex, rushing to stop him. But it was too late. As soon as the gap was wide enough, the four implings shot out of the darkness and took to the air. Her father stumbled backward in surprise, dropping the hatch. Immediately the imp spread its leathery wings and took off after its offspring.

"Alexandra, what . . . is this?" her father muttered, following the airborne parade of hell beasts with his eyes. They darted around the rafters in a line, her father's familiar taking up the rear. An expression of wonder blossomed across his face.

"The imp wasn't sick after all," Alex said. She was relieved that none of the implings seemed interested in attacking them. She took a moment to breathe. "It was in labor."

"In labor? As in with child? Why . . . this is wonderful," he said, smiling. "Now you can have a familiar of your very own!"

Oh, hell no! thought Alex. She wanted nothing to do with any of the creatures. One imp was nightmare enough!

A gout of flame appeared above them, accompanied by an unsettling screech. Alex looked up and was horrified by what she saw. The trailing impling was ablaze and squirming within the imp's mouth. The imp's teeth closed down upon it and, with a sickening crunch, snapped the impling in two, extinguishing its fires. The imp then devoured the unfortunate creature in midair.

The reaction from the other implings was instantaneous. They broke formation, each of them darting in different directions, each of them summoning their protective flames. Their screeches were horrendous.

"Wait! Stop!" cried her father as chaos erupted all around them.

The imp ignored him, dashing madly about in pursuit of its fleeing children. Small fires erupted everywhere the implings touched down. One by one, the imp caught, killed, and consumed each of its offspring, and by the time it was done, the whole barn was ablaze.

Alex couldn't believe what was happening. She stood there in shock. Her whole world was burning down around her.

"Alexandra, it's time for us to go!" her father said excitedly. He rushed to a nearby wall and began brushing aside a pile of hay. From it he retrieved a book, a staff, and a serpent-shaped bracelet.

"But what about the imp?" she asked, shaking off her stupor. The smoke was getting thick around them, and Alex could already feel the heat of the flames.

"He'll find us," her father replied. "He always does."

They ran out of the barn and into the fresh afternoon air. The breeze felt cool on Alex's face. Her father pointed to Jonathan's wagon and he bolted toward it, Alex following closely behind. The horses pranced nervously as they approached.

"Climb aboard—quickly," her father instructed. He placed both arms around her waist and hoisted her onto the wooden bench. He ran around to the other side, tossed his staff into the back, and jumped into the driver's seat. As soon as they were both settled, her father snapped the reins, and the horses began to move. Her father led them in a circle until they were facing the opposite direction. Another snap of the reins, and they were off.

Alex felt numb, as if she had just woken from a nightmare. It would take time to process the last day and a half. She glanced back at the burning building one final time. She knew it would be only a matter of moments before Widow Murphy realized that her barn was ablaze and that her brother's wagon was gone. She would blame Alex and her father for everything of course, but to be fair, they *were* to blame. They had brought the imp to her property after all. Alex was just relieved to be leaving this place and its unfriendly people behind.

"Where will we go?" she asked, turning back to her father.

"I'm not sure," he replied. Alex could tell that he too was shaken by the afternoon's events. "Let's head north, along the coast. There's a town called Salem that I'd like to check out."

Alex nodded, wondering what adventures awaited them there.

Later that evening . . .

Widow Murphy tossed aside the coverlet and jumped out of bed. She moved to the window and, pushing it open, leaned outside for a breath of fresh air. Her efforts were met with disappointment, however. Everything still smelled of smoke! She stepped back and stared angrily out at the darkness.

Rage coursed through her body. The widow had never been so upset in her life. Her two ungrateful farmhands had burned her barn to the ground, stolen her brother's wagon, and fled. And she had been so generous with them! How dare they repay her kindness with such vile behavior?

Her daughter Rebecca believed they had torched the barn out of jealousy and spite—and she tended to agree. People could be so petty. She wouldn't let them get away with it of course. In the morning, she'd head into Boston and speak with the authorities. They would act immediately, and her former farmhands would be found and made to pay. For the moment, however, she was in desperate need of sleep. Tomorrow was a new day.

Just as Widow Murphy was about to close the window, she noticed a flash of orange light off in the distance. Her curiosity piqued, she watched it for a moment as it danced on the horizon. It was too late in the year for fireflies, she knew. What else it could be, she couldn't imagine.

Gradually, the light grew larger. She stood transfixed by the glowing orange oddity heading her way. And then suddenly, just as quickly as it appeared, the light was gone. Her eyes scanned the darkness, but she found nothing. Had it been her imagination? She didn't think so.

Her ears soon registered an odd chirping sound that seemed to grow louder by the second. She squinted, struggling for signs of activity in the blackness outside until, finally, she sensed movement. A fluttering of wings?

A wave of anxiety washed over her. Something was hovering just outside the window! A blinding flash of light sent her stumbling backward, and when her eyes adjusted, she saw the nightmarish creature. Panic took hold, freezing Widow Murphy in place. Bulging eyes stared at her from an all too human face. Flames danced across the beast's small body as it bobbed in the air on bat-like wings. It smiled, revealing a mouth full of dripping, needlelike teeth. She gasped as it shot toward her through the open window.

Widow Murphy screamed.

Jenn: Part IV

Jenn spent the rest of the afternoon hanging out with Nate and Alex at the mansion. Zach was off running errands with his parents, which was fine with Jenn—their longtime relationship had begun to move out of the friend zone, and she was worried that it was happening too fast.

Jenn and the others listened to music on the third floor until Nate's brother, Marc, joined them for a movie. They watched *The Meg*, a film about a prehistoric shark that Jenn thought made *Jaws* seem like a dip in the kiddy pool. They hadn't seen Aunt Celia again and had learned nothing further about the old mirror. Around dinner time, Jenn's mother showed up to drive her home. Sometime later, when Jenn and her mother pulled into their driveway, Jenn was relieved to see no sign of the white owl. The creepy old bird was gone.

Jenn dreamed that night. She soared once again above the treetops as the town slept peacefully below. To her surprise, when she returned home, she saw the white owl sitting once again in the tree outside her bedroom window. She floated gracefully toward it, determined to find out what it was after.

"Hello," she said, floating vertically before it. It occurred to her that she looked like Superman in pajamas, suspended cape-less in midair. The bird just looked at her, its large orange eyes blinking once. "What do you want?" she asked. "Why are you following me?" Jenn wasn't expecting a response, so she was surprised when one came.

"Hello! I'm so happy you've come!" hooted the owl. "My name is Bubonivis. Your flying skills impressed me. I simply want to be your friend!"

What? Had she misinterpreted its intentions? Jenn wasn't sure what was stranger—that she understood its words or that the peculiar bird sought her companionship. *Only in a dream could something like this happen*, she thought. "But you've been stalking me," she said as she bobbed gently in the air. "And you left dead things all over my front steps!"

"Yes—I've been trying to get your attention," the owl hooted, then paused. "I'm so happy that it worked. And you are very welcome!"

"Welcome?" said Jenn.

"Yes," replied the owl. "You're welcome. I hope you enjoyed my surprise. I searched for hours, gathering only the most delicious of specimens! Were they tasty?"

What? Jenn's mouth fell open. Her forehead wrinkled and her stomach tightened. Only her fear of being rude kept her from gagging. "It was a gift? Oh, uh, I didn't realize. I—well—you *really* shouldn't have."

The bird's face beamed happiness. Jenn wasn't sure how she could tell.

"Oh, it was no problem at all," it replied excitedly, its talons digging into the thick branch on which it sat. "In fact, I'd be happy to hunt for more—"

"No!" interrupted Jenn. "That won't be necessary." Clearly, the owl hadn't seen her dispose of the dead animals that morning. She cringed. Jenn had never been so thankful for trash pickup day. "Listen, Bubonivis—"

"Oh! No need to be formal! Since we're becoming such good friends, you may call me Bob!"

Bob? Seriously? Good friends? Jenn could sense the bird's sudden, almost frenzied excitement. Its head spun nearly completely around in one direction, and then in the other. Jenn decided it was probably best to end the interaction. "Listen—Bob—thanks for your gift, but it's getting late. I really must be going."

"Oh, if you must." The owl appeared sad for a moment, but its unusual elation returned quickly. "I'm just thrilled that we've become so close!"

So close? Is this crazy bird serious? No, it couldn't be. None of this was even real—Jenn was dreaming, after all.

"Okay, then," she said, nodding at the bird. She flashed a weak smile. "Bob, it was nice meeting you. I have to go. Good night." She began to turn away when its enthusiastic hooting continued:

"Good night, my friend! Will I see you tomorrow night? I look forward to getting to know you. The more we chat, the more familiar I'll become with—"

The owl's chatter became a distant buzzing in Jenn's ear. Her mind suddenly began racing, her pulse pounding. She turned and flew off into the night. Jenn soared over and past her house with no clear destination in mind. She didn't know how far she flew, or even when the dream ended, but the next morning when she woke up, a single phrase echoed through her mind on repeat. She'd nearly choked when she'd heard the owl speak it. It had been just a fraction of the bird's parting words, but her mind was unable to move past it. The full statement had begun:

The more we chat, the more familiar I'll become—

The phrase Jenn's mind had homed in on was:

Familiar, I'll become.

Did the strangely obsessed white owl in her dream want to be her familiar? Was the real owl, the creature she'd found creepy and off-putting, there for the same purpose? The idea sent panic through Jenn's mind. She wasn't prepared for such an eventuality. What should she do? Jenn didn't have any answers, but she knew someone who might. She jumped out of bed and quickly pulled on some clothes.

Aunt Celia had told Jenn to drop by for help at any time. Once again, Jenn planned to take her up on that offer.

Jenn, Nate, and Aunt Celia sat around the table in Aunt Celia's artifact room.

"You spent yesterday afternoon placing protection wards around the basement?" asked Nate, repeating what Aunt Celia had just told them. "But why?"

Aunt Celia leaned forward. "It was very shortsighted of me not to do so when we set the original wards around the house," she replied. "My suspicion is that someone entered the cellar and placed the miniature mansion inside that small corridor for someone to find."

"But who would do that?" asked Nate. He tapped his fingers nervously on the tabletop, betraying his otherwise calm demeanor. "And why?"

"Also, *how* would someone do that?" Jenn added. "Is there an exit hatch down there?" She didn't remember seeing one from the outside.

Aunt Celia shook her head. "No, there is not. And I can't speak to the who or the why. It could be that Malleus Hodge left it before he was banished, but I don't think that's the case."

"Is this some new threat then?" Nate asked. He glanced between Aunt Celia and Jenn.

"It could be," said Aunt Celia, "but I've been grasping at straws. I spoke with Tee on the off chance that she left it as some sort of practical joke, but, of course, she knew nothing about it. She said she'd pop in later to help investigate, though."

Tee, aka Tituba, was an old friend of Aunt Celia's who also happened to be a witch. Jenn remembered the first time they'd met. The woman had arrived suddenly, appearing before them through magickal means. She'd brought her familiar, Neloye, with her. Neloye was a giant leopard whose appearance had caused a stir.

"In all likelihood," continued Aunt Celia, "we won't be able to determine who left it—for now at least." She turned to Jenn. "As for the *how*, I suspect it had something to do with the wall-sized mirror we found down there."

The mirror! thought Jenn. *No wonder Aunt Celia had seemed distressed by it.*

"What do you mean?" asked Nate. He inched his chair forward, his curiosity obviously stirred.

"Well," began Aunt Celia. "Let's just say that mirrors aren't simply light-wave reflectors." She stood and approached the door to the hall. When she closed it, Jenn saw the full-length mirror attached to its back.

"They can be so much more. A properly enchanted set of mirrors, for example, can act as a teleportation device, allowing a person to step into one and out of the other—no matter how far apart in distance they may physically be. They must be sizable enough for the person to pass through, of course."

Jenn nodded to herself, remembering Corvin's adventure with the gorgon. The mirrors in that story had been small, but it made sense that larger enchanted mirrors could exist as well.

"For a pair of mirrors to be magickally connected, however, they first must be in close physical proximity," continued Aunt Celia. "If our mirror has a counterpart, then the two mirrors would've had to have been joined ages ago, at some point prior to me living here. Also, I tested its surface, and it remains firm." She tapped on the glass of the mirror in front of her. "There are ways of locking enchanted mirrors so that they appear solid to the touch, but I doubt that's the case here."

"Then what are you thinking?" asked Nate.

"Well, as you know, *ghosts* can also pass into mirrors," she said, gesturing to the one on the door.

Jenn couldn't believe her ears—*ghosts?* She noticed that Nate didn't seem surprised by his aunt's words. He nodded in response.

"And any mirror will do. For them, the world behind the glass can act as a gateway—to other mirrors, sometimes even to other realities or planes of existence."

Whoa, thought Jenn. She found this information troubling and burdensome. As a firm believer in science, she was unable to wrap her head around such a mind-numbing concept.

"You think a ghost is behind this?" asked Nate. His brows were raised, and he looked worried.

Aunt Celia shrugged. "I really don't know. But it's possible."

Jenn remained silent as she tried to process her thoughts. She felt almost relieved when a loud growl from a distant part of the house cut through the silence. To Jenn it sounded like the MGM lion that she'd seen at the start of so many old movies.

"I think Tee has arrived," said Aunt Celia with a grin.

And with that, the topic of ghosts, for the time being, was forgotten.

"Jenn, I'd like to talk to Nate for a moment," said Aunt Celia. "Why don't you go down and say hello to Tee? I filled her in on your encounters with the white owl. She has good advice to offer, especially on the acquisition of familiars." She punctuated the sentence with a wink. Her warm expression told Jenn that this meeting with Tee had been planned all along.

"Sure," said Jenn. With a nod, she smiled. "I'll do that." She stood, pushed in her chair, and headed for the hallway. Jenn was eager to hear what Tee had to say on the subject of familiars. She respected the woman as much as she respected Aunt Celia. If Tee could help her sort out her latest dream and the real-life owl's intentions, it would go a long way in helping her to understand her own feelings on the matter.

Jenn hurried down the grand staircase to the first-floor foyer. A soft rumbling directed her to the left where the living room's double doorway stood open, its large sliding doors stashed deeply within their narrow wall pockets. She walked in to find Tee smiling, standing there amid the antiques. The woman wore a flowing outfit of yellows and oranges that perfectly complimented her flawless dark skin. Her hair was tied back in a colorful ribbon that accentuated her long golden earrings.

"Jenn, my dear," she said, her grin growing wider. She opened her arms invitingly.

"Hello, Tee," said Jenn, stepping toward her and accepting the hug. The woman smelled of fresh air and spices, a scent Jenn remembered from their last visit. Tee's warm embrace had a calming effect that put Jenn at ease. "It's nice to see you again. I—"

Jenn was startled by a loud growl. Over Tee's shoulder, along the far wall, she saw Neloye, Tee's giant feline familiar. The leopard had made itself at home on one of Aunt Celia's fancy upholstered sofas.

"Wait your turn, girl!" Tee scolded the large cat. As she broke their embrace, Tee whispered into Jenn's ear: "I believe Neloye's developed a bad case of FOMO recently."

Fear of missing out? thought Jenn. *For real? Did all familiars develop human characteristics?*

Before Jenn could verbalize her question, Tee turned to the animal. "Don't worry, Neloye! Jenn will hug you too!" she said in a reassuring voice.

I will? Jenn, for her part, wasn't reassured at all. Her heart began to beat faster.

"She doesn't like being ignored," Tee whispered softly so that only Jenn could hear.

"I—er—can see that," she replied. The leopard was grooming itself with its large, rough tongue. It was purring once again, producing the same deep rumbling that had attracted Jenn to the living room. Although she had met Neloye before, she was not yet comfortable around the creature. Did Tee really expect her to hug the beast?

"Go on," said Tee. She smiled and gestured toward the cat. "Go say hello!"

Apparently, Tee expected just that. Jenn took several cautious steps in Neloye's direction, turning back once to look at Tee, who nodded encouragingly for her to continue. When she reached the sofa, she knelt by the leopard, wondering if she should wait for it to acknowledge her. Again Jenn glanced at Tee, and again Tee nodded for her to continue.

Jenn placed her hand gently on the leopard's soft, furry ribcage. Almost immediately, a sense of calm overtook Jenn. Other feelings washed over her, feelings of love, fierce loyalty, and pride—feelings that she knew belonged to Neloye. It was as if their physical contact had, somehow, connected them emotionally. *How is that possible?* she wondered.

Jenn was awed by the experience. She felt the rise and fall of Neloye's breathing, each exhale accented by the creature's thrumming purrs. Not only could she sense the majestic creature itself, but Jenn could sense echoes of Tee as well—the woman's strength, her wisdom, her kindness, and above all else, her love for Neloye.

Jenn felt a tickle on her cheek as the cat's whiskers grazed her skin. Before she realized what was happening, Neloye's large, purring face pressed firmly into Jenn's chest, knocking her off balance. Reflexively, Jenn wrapped her arm around the leopard's neck to keep herself upright. It continued to bat Jenn around with its playful, powerful skull. Jenn tightened her embrace accordingly, scratching the animal's head with her free hand. Jenn couldn't help but laugh at the joy she felt over the unexpected interaction. She gazed at the creature, overcome by its magnificence—no, Jenn corrected herself, by *her* magnificence; Neloye no longer seemed like a simple animal to her—and by the equally incredible connection that the large familiar shared with Tee. Jenn looked back at Tee and smiled.

"She's wonderful, isn't she?" said Tee. "Neloye and I have been together so long now that I couldn't imagine a life without her."

"Yes. I can tell that your relationship is very strong—and very close. Do all familiars have close bonds with their masters?"

"Oh, I am not Neloye's master," said Tee with a shake of the head. "Neloye and I are very much equals. Although our bond is magickal in nature, we have a relationship based upon mutual respect. I would never enforce my will upon her. Most witches do become quite close to their familiars. It's the strong emotional connection we share." Tee tapped her temple with a finger. "There are no secrets between us, and that is the basis for any strong, long-lasting relationship."

"That makes sense," said Jenn. She rose to her feet, giving Neloye a final scratch between the ears. Neloye went back to grooming her paws. "Aunt Celia's and Corvin's relationship is like that too, isn't it?"

"Yes, it is." Tee smiled knowingly. She waved Jenn over to a nearby loveseat and the two women sat. "Celia told me about your white owl." She placed her hand on Jenn's knee. "I do not know if the owl is looking to become your familiar. What I can tell you, however, is that if it's meant to be, it will be."

Meant to be? Was Tee telling her that she had no say in the matter? That wasn't the kind of advice she was hoping to hear. "But I'm not even sure I want a familiar!" she said.

Tee smiled reassuringly. "That decision will be entirely up to you. But any relationship you develop with a familiar—or potential familiar—will happen naturally, organically. You'll know what to do when the time comes. I found Neloye during my travels abroad, and it was immediately evident to both of us that our paths were aligned. Celia found Corvin as a fledgling with a broken wing. She nursed him back to health, and gradually, over the years, their relationship grew. There is no one specific way to obtain a familiar—and if you decide you don't want one, that's fine too." Jenn felt a sense of relief at Tee's words.

"One thing I *will* say," Tee continued, "is that it's a relationship like no other."

Jenn felt certain that truer words had never been spoken.

An excited yapping sound drew her attention. It was coming from outside the room and growing louder and closer by the moment. Through the open doorway burst Blaze, Marc's new puppy. The dog ran into the room's center, its full attention focused on Neloye. Baring tiny fangs, Blaze released a long, low growl.

The leopard responded with a startlingly ferocious hiss. Moving slowly, menacingly, Neloye placed one paw on the floor and then another, stepping gingerly off the sofa until she stood towering over the excited canine. Jenn realized that Blaze didn't stand a chance against the larger creature, and her pulse quickened. Against her better judgement, she began to rise from the loveseat—The touch of Tee's hand on her forearm held her back. Jenn glanced at the older woman, who responded with a quick shake of the head. Tee clearly felt it best not to interfere.

The two animals stared intently at each other as if each were daring the other to make the first move. Blaze released a howl and then leaped forward—just as Neloye pounced. Jenn watched in horror as the leopard, teeth bared, came down on top of the tiny puppy.

And that was when Blaze's body began to change. The dog's size grew tenfold in a matter of seconds. Jenn scrambled backward, climbing onto the back of the loveseat as the creatures collided, their momentum sending them sideways in an awkward tumble.

What the hell? Jenn couldn't believe her eyes.

The animals rolled about the floor for a moment, Neloye seemingly gaining the upper hand—until Blaze suddenly burst into flame! Blue fire erupted from the now-giant dog's legs, back, and head.

"Oh my god!" Jenn managed as her heart kicked into higher gear. "Tee, what—" Aghast, Jenn glanced at Tee in time to see the woman raise her arm into the air. With the slightest flick of the wrist, the sprawling oriental rug beneath the tussling creatures vanished, leaving only the equally sprawling hardwood floor.

Jenn's mouth fell open at Tee's unusual and unexpected display of magick.

Blaze regained his feet and leaped for Neloye, sending the two of them careening for an antique table with a crystal vase of fresh flowers. Tee gestured once again and the table, vase, and flowers vanished. Neloye and Blaze rolled through the vacated area, bouncing off the wall before tumbling in the opposite direction, a whirlwind of legs, teeth, fire, and claws. As soon as they'd moved on, the table and its contents returned unblemished, courtesy of Tee's teleportation magick. Jenn looked at the older woman, surprised to see the wide, amused smile now brightening her face.

"They like to roughhouse," said Tee, returning Jenn's confused gaze. "Sometimes the dog wins, sometimes the cat."

Roughhouse?

By this time, Neloye had gained the advantage—in fact, it appeared as though she had won the battle. The fiery canine lay upside down, pinned beneath the leopard's muscular body. Neloye ran a damp tongue across Blaze's squirming face. The blue flame seemed to have no effect on Neloye. After a moment, she released Blaze, and both creatures rose calmly to their feet, neither of them showing signs of aggression or permanent damage.

Jenn's wide-eyed gaze traveled from the animals to Tee as her heartbeat began to slow. "What just happened? And—and—what *is* he?" Jenn turned and pointed at Blaze, stunned to see that the puppy had returned to its original size. It stood silently beside Neloye, blue flames still rising from its small body. Both the canine and the feline stared back at her, as if trying to determine what the fuss was about. As she watched, Blaze's flames died away. Several minor scorch marks on the floor were the only evidence that they'd ever existed.

Without a word, Tee rose, stepping quickly over to one of the marks. She rubbed the tip of her shoe across it and frowned when it didn't wipe away. "Oops," she said, looking at Jenn with a shrug. She gestured and the oriental rug reappeared beneath them, concealing the blemishes from view.

"He's no ordinary dog," said Jenn as she waited for Tee to say something further. She remembered that it was, in fact, Tee who had given the puppy to Nate's brother.

"No," said Tee. "He isn't. He's part hellhound—but only one-eighth! Allie—er, Celia still hasn't let me off the hook for that. Anyway, he and Neloye are old pals."

A hellhound? thought Jenn. Her eyes widened. *As in a hound from Hell? Nothing is ever ordinary around here!*

"In spite of Celia's misgivings, that dog will make a fine familiar for someone someday, I think," Tee added with a wink. "But enough of that. Let's return to the topic of you and the white owl." She returned to her spot on the antique loveseat. "As I said before, I don't know what the future holds for you—but I will say that having the right familiar can enhance your life in ways you could never imagine. A familiar can offer love and companionship, protection and guidance. A familiar could, one day, even save your life."

"Save my life?" Jenn's heart rate had returned to normal, and she was interested in hearing more.

"Yes. Neloye has saved my life on numerous occasions." Tee thought for a moment. "I know, let me tell you the story of the time Neloye and I met the Pendle witch."

Jenn nodded, intrigued. She slid off the back of the loveseat, and as they made themselves comfortable, Jenn noticed that Neloye had returned to the sofa. The leopard's chest rose and fell as she dozed. Blaze slept curled up beside her, the small dog's body nestled between the giant cat's paws. *Two very unusual beasts,* she thought. The scene warmed Jenn's heart, and she smiled. When she turned back to Tee, the older woman was smiling as well.

"Let's begin, shall we?" said Tee. "The year was, let me think—1760 . . ."

Tituba and The Pendle Witch

By Joseph J. Christiano

At the Border, October 1760

It was the dream that bade her to leave her home in the middle of the night. Or perhaps it was no dream at all. Whatever it was that woke her, that drenched her night clothes in sweat, it had originated far from her temporary residence in Springfield in the Massachusetts Bay Colony. She did not know how she knew, not precisely; these feelings came to her at odd times, and there was no method to predict when and how they would arrive. All Tituba knew was that something was . . . off.

These feelings usually meant the presence of a magickal artifact. She had decided half a century ago that it would be wise to study and collect such trinkets. Were she called upon to defend herself from dark sorcery—and not for the first time—it would do to have as much help as possible. She had collected several items and studied their properties. Those she deemed to be of use, she kept. Others were gifted to people she knew to have an interest in such things.

Tituba could not remember the dream/vision, not in any meaningful way. She recalled almost nothing, just a vague sense of where it had taken her. It was south, somewhere within the Connecticut Colony. She used her magick to position herself at the border. She might have traveled farther; the limit of her ability had yet to present itself. For all she knew, she could appear in the heart of London if she so wished. But it also left her fatigued, and she felt she might need her strength. So it was a short jump, perhaps ten miles at most. She arrived with just a slight headache that vanished after a few moments.

Before her stretched the wilderness of northern Connecticut. The sun was rising, and the trees, all orange and red with the approach of autumn, welcomed the end of night. Tituba less so. She was no man's property, not any longer, but the people she was certain to encounter would suspect her of escape. At best she could count upon a cold welcome. At worst . . .

She started walking. There were several paths through the forest, and Tituba chose the one that appeared the least traveled. If she could manage to avoid strangers on the road, so much the better. After a few hours, she stopped to pick some berries, and she sat by a stream and ate them and sipped water. She had left her home with nothing but a few pieces of hardtack, and the berries were a welcome addition to her diet. She rested by the stream until she felt the soreness leave her feet, and then she was moving again.

By noon, she caught the sound of civilization somewhere ahead. She slowed her pace. The forest was still thick enough that she could conceal her presence, and she used it for that precise purpose. The sounds grew louder as she advanced. Tituba bent down when she saw the end of the woods ahead of her. She caught a glimpse of what she took to be a church. Several people walked by, while others were engaged in conversation in front of the building. Around it, several homes and shops came into view.

She saw several Africans among the populace. All appeared to be property, carrying heavy sacks of whatever their masters gave them to deliver to other masters. Tituba frowned. Memories of her time with Samuel Parris returned to her—not that those thoughts were ever very far away. But Parris was long dead, as were all who knew him. She tossed aside the image of her former master and again regarded the town.

She got no sense of anything magickal nearby. Whatever it was that woke her from her sound sleep was not here. Tituba kept her distance from the tree line and skirted the settlement.

She took only one chance. At the village's southern border stood one last house. It was large, larger than any she had seen in Salem Town, but well shy of some of the estates in Boston. On the near side of the house sat five large baskets. Each was full of apples and pears. Seeing no one about, Tituba broke from the tree line and made for the baskets.

She started to tip over the last one, thought better of it, and took a few apples and stuffed them into her skirts. Then she upended the basket. Its contents spilled onto the grass. Tituba grabbed the basket and hurried back to the tree line.

She walked south for the next twenty minutes before she stopped. A good-sized rock sat in a partial clearing. Tituba sat upon the rock and ate her pilfered goods. The apples were ripe, sweet, and she devoured them. It beat the hell out of the hardtack in her pack.

Her belly full of sweet fruit, she started south again, the basket slung over her shoulder. The woods became thicker, and low branches began to tug at her skirts. Tituba turned east toward the sound of horses and wagons that she had followed for some time.

The road was wide enough to accommodate two carriages abreast of each other. The dirt was well-worn and packed tightly beneath her feet. She grasped the basket with both hands and set off down the road. The next settlement of any size would be Hartford. With luck she could make it there before dark.

Perhaps two hours later, she saw and heard a carriage approaching from the south. Drawn by four horses, it was a large, garish contraption. One man sat at the front, reins grasped firmly within his strong hands. The gait of the horses was moderate, steady. Tituba moved to the edge of the road and continued walking.

The driver pulled up on the reins as the carriage neared the newcomer. The carriage ground to a halt. The driver regarded Tituba with a squint and a sneer. "What are you doing out here by yourself?"

Tituba hefted the empty basket. "On m'way to Hartford, sir. Pick up some wheat and tobacco for the master." Tituba was of mixed ancestry. Because she was dark skinned, people believed her to be simple-minded and illiterate. She felt no need to disabuse them of that fact. She was no fool—the world was unfair to people like her, and Tituba had no problem with taking advantage of their idiotic assumptions.

The man with the reins spat onto the ground. "You wouldn't be trying to escape, would you?"

Tituba did her best to act surprised. "Oh, no, sir! I would *never* do that! My master, he treats me good! You can ask him yourself when you get to town."

"And who might own you, woman?"

Tituba kept the sneer from her lips but only just. *No one owns me, you old fool,* she thought. *I'd love to demonstrate that fact, but you're not worth the effort.* "Hodge be the master's name, sir. Mat—Math—Matthew Hodge." She considered the stutter a perfect touch.

"I'll be calling on your master when I get there. If I find out you lied to me—"

"No lie, sir! I swears!"

A man poked his head out the side window of the carriage just then. "Why are we sitting here, Mr. Platt? I have a schedule to keep. Speak to this slave on your own time!" The man's head disappeared back inside the carriage.

The horseman's lips turned down in a sneer. Clearly, he disliked the man in the carriage. He seemed to like Tituba even less. "I'll call on your master," he repeated. Then he whipped the reins, and the horse started forward again.

Tituba watched them depart. She smiled, returned the basket to its former place over her shoulder, and continued south.

Neloye and the Wolves

She did indeed reach Hartford before nightfall. The wind had picked up, banishing the warmth of the day and reminding her it was autumn. Tituba was tired, her feet and legs were sore, and she had had just about enough of carrying the basket. Even empty, its weight seemed to increase as the hours and miles went past.

She passed several taverns on what she took to be the main road in the town. Light and laughter spilled from them, a reminder she was alone. She could not enter one, of course; the basket was a great prop for hiding her status as a free woman, but it would do nothing to get her a roof over her head . . . or to fill her belly.

She found a farmer's field not far from the main road and sat at its edge by the tree line and ate her hardtack. As hard and tasteless as the bread was, she had eaten worse. When she finished, she sat back and whistled softly. As expected, Neloye made her presence known immediately. Never far away, the great cat emerged from the woods at Tituba's back. It approached her and sniffed about the area. Apparently satisfied that they were alone, the leopard sat in front of her and licked her face.

"Thank you, girl. I could use the love." She patted the cat's head, ran her hand down Neloye's smooth back, and tugged playfully at her tail. Neloye placed a giant paw on Tituba's shoulder, which almost knocked her to the ground. Tituba laughed, and the big cat lowered herself onto Tituba's body. "Oof!" Tituba mock-cried. "You're trying to crush me, you big baby!" Neloye responded by licking her face again. "I love you too," Tituba told her.

They played for a while more before the weariness of the day proved too much. Sleeping in the open, in an unfamiliar place, was not the smartest decision she could make, but the presence of her familiar put her at ease. Tituba used her pack as a pillow, and she closed her eyes and slept. And dreamed.

She dreamed of the artifact, as she suspected she might. She could not see what it was, only that it was small, perhaps the size of a lantern, and black as midnight. Had the dream ended there, she would have been no closer to its location. But the dream did not end there. Tituba also saw a town. Houses of good size, many fields of crops, a small, narrow stream that meandered its way through the area. The town appeared to be in a valley that stretched over the horizon. There was a statue as well. She couldn't make it out, not in any great detail, but she knew it was of a man, one dressed in clothing at least one hundred years out of date. An old statue, perhaps the town's founder or some other person of reverence. She might have gotten more detail had she not been awakened by a low growl from Neloye.

Tituba's eyes snapped open. She was fully awake instantly. She sat up and her head whipped about, seeking the cause of the leopard's alarm.

Six wolves stood just this side of the tree line. They stood shoulder to shoulder as if they were soldiers about to march into battle. They growled, their teeth bared. Their eyes were narrowed and focused on the big leopard. Neloye growled back, and the hair along her spine stood at attention.

"Easy, girl," Tituba whispered. She crawled on her hands and knees until she reached Neloye. "Easy. Give them a minute to think it over."

If the wolves took the opportunity, they did not show it. They advanced as one, growling, saliva dripping from bared fangs.

"Are you sure you want to do this?" Tituba asked them. "This will not result in full bellies for you. It might for Neloye."

Neloye crouched, her muscles coiled and begging for release. One of the wolves got too close, and the leopard received her wish. Neloye moved too quickly for Tituba to follow. The great cat crashed into the first wolf. The animal bounced back from the impact and rolled across the ground for several feet. It sprang up, growling, its fur standing straight up. Neloye took the opportunity to lunge at two of its companions. Apparently smarter than their brethren, these two retreated past the edge of the tree line and were gone.

One of the remaining wolves managed to outflank the leopard and approached Tituba. She regarded the foolish intruder with a smile. It lunged for her . . . and caught empty air. Tituba was not there. The animal landed ungracefully, but regained its feet in an instant. It looked about until its eyes settled on Tituba, now standing twenty feet away.

"Not this evening, sir," Tituba told it. "Nor any other. Best to leave before Neloye becomes angry."

It was at that moment Neloye sprang upon the poor beast. Her greater weight forced the wolf to the ground. Neloye placed her jaws around the wolf's throat and growled. Her eyes found the remaining three wolves still on this side of the tree line, and she held their gaze. They pranced back and forth, lifting their front legs as if they were horses rearing up.

Tituba tensed, ready to apparate again if one of the other wolves tried for her. Instead, the three near the tree line turned and bolted into the woods, leaving the last one behind.

Tituba approached Neloye and the remaining wolf and placed her hand on the leopard's shoulder. "He learned his lesson, I think, girl. He'll trouble us no longer."

Neloye growled again and released the wolf from her jaws. She stood between it and Tituba, ready to lunge should the beast try again. It bared its teeth one last time and bolted for the woods.

Tituba breathed a sigh of relief. She took a deep breath, felt the cold night air invade her lungs. She stood there until her heart slowed its pace and the great cat had once again lain down at her feet. Tituba sat. "Well, that interruption cost me the location of the artifact, Neloye. If we're threatened again, try to protect me a little more quietly."

The leopard groaned her reply.

Done Pretending

Tituba did not dream again that night, and so she remained no closer to locating the artifact. In the morning, she let Neloye roam the woods while she set off south, her pilfered basket once more on her shoulder. It came in handy twice more; once outside Farmington with a man much like Mr. Platt, and another along the main road in Harwinton. Each time she gave the name of a settlement to the north, and each time she came up with another fake name for another fake master. Most people she encountered didn't bother with her at all. Most refused to even acknowledge her. That was just fine. Tituba decided long ago she did not want attention.

Her second night on the road found her in another open field bordered by woods. Neloye returned and stood guard—or slept through the night, Tituba could not be sure—and this time Tituba got through most of the dream uninterrupted.

She stood in a town square, a wide dirt road going in both directions around her. In front of her stood the statue. She got a better look at it this time. It was of a man in the garb of an Elizabethan explorer. His plumed tunic gave the appearance of royalty or, at least, nobility. His trusted musket stood at his side, his left hand resting on the stock. In his right hand he held a book. There was writing engraved upon the statue's granite base. Tituba actually tried to hide that she could read it before she remembered this was a dream.

ROBERT JAMES DEACON

it read. And below that, in smaller letters, *Founded 1698*.

The name meant nothing to her, nor the area around the statue. Wherever this artifact was hiding, it was some place she had never visited before. She awoke feeling rested and determined. Now that she had another clue as to the artifact's whereabouts, Tituba wanted to be on the move immediately.

Biological necessity bade otherwise, and she forced herself to eat more of the hardtack—running low now—and sip water from the nearby stream. Neloye greeted her, and she spent a few moments with the leopard before telling her they were getting closer to their destination. Tituba didn't know this for a fact, but she felt it was true.

By midafternoon, she had entered the town of South Farmington. She smiled warmly at the Africans she saw running this way and that as they toiled for their masters. None returned her smile. Seeing them made her think of Parris again. And as was always the case, Tituba pushed memories of the old bastard from her mind. He was in the ground and so were his children. She could not think of a better place for him.

Walking through South Farmington proved a fortuitous decision on Tituba's part. The town's center displayed a large map of the Colony of Connecticut. Tituba scanned the image for anything that resembled a valley. She found it west of the Connecticut River. "Naugatuck Valley," she whispered as she read the name. Her finger traced the path of the valley south and then stopped abruptly. There, north and west of a town called Waterbury, sat a place called Deacon's Landing. "Robert James Deacon," she said aloud. She smiled. *Now I have a destination.*

"Were you reading that?"

Tituba started. She spun, saw a man and a woman standing perhaps ten feet from her. His expression was hard, not quite angry but certainly getting close. His female companion regarded Tituba with open contempt.

"I—I—" *I was stupid,* she finished the thought. *Reading in public. You'd better wake up, girl. This isn't Barbados.*

"Who taught you to read, girl?" the man demanded. "Don't just stand there. Answer me!"

"Fetch the constable," the woman suggested.

"An excellent idea," the man declared. He leveled a finger at Tituba. "You stay right there. We'll get to the bottom of this and make no mistake!"

The moment they were out of view, Tituba apparated to the other side of town. If anyone saw her disappear into thin air, she did not care. The last thing she needed was to run afoul of the law. A slave—even a former slave, now free—was not allowed to read. She had nearly blown it, but now she was clear of the man and his wife and she had the information she needed.

Tituba started down the road, stopped, looked at the basket. She found herself hating this thing of woven wicker that smelled of old fruit. She hated that she had needed it several times already and would most likely need it again. With a grunt, she hurled it into a farmer's field by the side of the road. She was done pretending. She was also done hiding her abilities. If she ran into trouble again, of the human or animal kind, she would simply disappear from their view. She could imagine the calls of "witch!" that might follow, as they had so many times in the past. Tituba was beyond caring. Let them come.

She continued south until she found herself looking down at the heavy forest that made up this part of the Naugatuck Valley.

Bad Dreams

Neloye returned when Tituba entered the forest. She had calmed somewhat after the affair with the man and his wife. She had decided to avoid roads as much as possible from here to Deacon's Landing and the mysterious magickal artifact it held. The leopard was pleased to see her and nuzzled her hand whenever Tituba paused to sip water from the stream. When Tituba stopped to sit upon a rock and eat more of the hardtack, Neloye plopped herself down and rested her head on Tituba's feet. That evening, far from the road where no sounds of civilization reached them, Tituba chanced a fire to drive away the October chill. The fire drew insects, and she used her magick to send them to South Farmington where she hoped they would dine on the old fool and his wife.

She thought back to the map. Deacon's Landing was almost due west of her current location. From what she could remember, there were not many settlements between here and there. She should be able to stick to the forest most of the way. With luck, and if she managed to get some sleep, she would be there by noon tomorrow.

She dreamed of the statue again. It appeared to her with such clarity it was as if she were standing directly in front of it. The artifact, whatever it was, was connected to the statue. Buried beneath it, perhaps, or entombed within the stone itself. She still could not make out what it was or what power it possessed, but it was no mere trinket, of that she was certain.

In the dream, day turned to night, and Tituba tilted her head up and regarded the sky. Clouds as black as obsidian rolled across the sun and blotted it from existence. Something darker, blacker, moved within those clouds. She could not see what it was, nor did she want to. It was big, bigger even than the whales she had seen in Barbados when she was a child, and it moved with a grace that defied nature.

An appendage of some sort—it was impossibly long and thick and moved as if it were liquid—descended from the black clouds. Its passage over her head created a burst of wind that tore at her clothes, her skin. Tituba ducked out of its way although the limb passed more than a mile above her. The thing in the clouds roared, and Tituba clenched her eyes shut and covered her ears. She felt the ground beneath her feet undulate as if she were standing upon the ocean. Tituba shrieked, but for the roar above, she could not hear her own voice. After several moments, the sound died as suddenly as it was birthed. The entirety of the world became still, as if the thing above the clouds had ceased to exist.

She opened her eyes and saw a realm the likes of which she had never seen. Buildings bigger than anything even in Boston, made of glass and stone and metal, surrounded her. Most were in ruins, and flames danced among the debris. The smoke was thick and stung her eyes. It billowed into the sky and blotted out all the light. Bodies lay scattered about her. None moved. Tituba gasped and coughed as the smoke invaded her lungs. She collapsed to her knees.

"What . . . ?" She did not know what she saw, had never seen structures such as those. Even in ruin, they spoke of power and a skill to build that did not yet exist. The future? Her dreams had never shown her anything of that sort before. The influence of the artifact, possibly. It may be far more powerful than she had surmised.

With a flash of bright light, the ruined necropolis vanished, and she was back in Deacon's Landing. The sky remained black as pitch, but she could see no movement within the clouds. Whatever it was that had revealed itself to her was gone.

Tituba returned her gaze to the statue, and she found it was likewise gone. In its place stood a man, his features concealed within a robe of yellow. Tituba gasped and took a quick step back. She was not fast enough. The man raised his arm, and his hand affixed itself to her throat. Tituba struggled but the man's strength far exceeded hers. He pulled her closer to his concealed face. Tituba knew she wanted to be no closer to the apparition, so she apparated . . . but her magick failed her. She remained in the man's grip. As he pulled her ever closer, she could see his lips turn up in a smile. His teeth were black and filed to sharp points.

"He wants you," the man told her. He stretched out each word. Tituba tried to scream but found herself incapable of even that; the man's hand may as well have been made of granite. He pulled her in until all the world consisted of the robe and the hidden face within.

Tituba screamed and sat bolt upright. Her lungs gulped air, her hair was pasted to her skull with sweat, her eyes wide and wild. Neloye leaped to her feet and growled, her eyes scanning every direction for the threat. Nothing presented itself, and the leopard looked at Tituba as if to ask, *What was that about?*

Tituba placed her hand over her heart, felt it slamming against the inside of her ribcage. With conscious effort, she slowed her breathing. It took several moments before her heart decided it liked it better inside her body and stopped trying to burst out. Her breathing returned to almost normal. It was only then she remembered the familiar at her side. She petted the leopard, and it licked her hand. "Sorry, girl. Bad dreams."

It occurred to her she could still taste the smoke she had swallowed in her dream. Its residue coated her tongue and her throat, and she coughed. She fancied she could actually see some of it exit her body through her mouth and nose. Or perhaps it was simply the chill of the night air. She could not be certain.

Neloye nuzzled her again, clearly confused about what had just happened. Tituba scratched behind the leopard's ear, and Neloye laid on the ground and rolled onto her side. Tituba rubbed her belly and smiled at her. But her thoughts were on the man in the yellow robe. If he was there when she reached the statue . . . what? What would she do? Tituba hoped she would not have to answer that question.

Welcome to Deacon's Landing

It was just after noon when Tituba reached the outskirts of Deacon's Landing. From her vantage point atop a hill, she saw the town stretched out below her. It reminded her of Salem Village, although it was less than half the size. The houses were few and far between and fairly large for what looked to be a farming community. The public houses were larger still, and people walked this way and that.

Her hand rubbed behind Neloye's ear. "You'd better stay here, girl. I doubt these people would welcome a big kitty like you into their town." She thought about it. "They probably feel the same way about me." The leopard purred and licked her hand.

Tituba descended the hill. The first few people who noticed her ignored her. She eyed them suspiciously. She had expected questions, and she had an answer at the ready. She had a similar reaction from everyone she came across. Some ignored her, some greeted her with a tilt of the head. A few men even doffed their caps. No one stopped her or questioned her presence.

She passed a general store that seemed to be quite busy. There stood a smithy where the blacksmiths pounded out their wares. There was even an office for a doctor. Her attention was drawn to a darker, somewhat shabby building. It stood down the street at the edge of the town. Curious, she approached it. A Chinese man—the first one Tituba had seen in person in many years—stood outside, smoking his pipe. The smoke smelled like nothing Tituba had encountered before. Something about it made her uneasy. He smiled and indicated the door behind him with a tilt of his head. Tituba retreated back the way she had come.

She scanned the short side streets until she saw the largest building she had thus far come across. It stood on the next street over. She walked down the side street until the large building was in front of her. *The town hall,* she thought. It could not be anything else. Two full stories, large windows across both floors, two ornate doors at the top of sturdy wooden steps. Multiple people walked in and out and went about their business. In front of the building, in the center of the street, stood the statue from her dreams.

Tituba approached it. The detail was remarkable, but that in itself was all the statue had to offer. It depicted Robert James Deacon, presumably the founder of the settlement, standing bravely with his musket by his side. She reached out and placed her hand on the statue, felt the cold black stone beneath her palm. She sensed nothing out of the ordinary.

"You're hiding something, my friend," she told the long-dead man. *If I were a necromancer, I could just ask him.* The thought both made her smile and horrified her. She had seen a necromancer in action only once, and that was enough for her. She felt fortunate she did not possess that particular ability.

Tituba closed her eyes. Her hand traveled down the front of the cold stone. When it reached the granite base, she knelt and continued her way down.

"I knew it would draw someone like you sooner or later."

Tituba's eyes flew open at the sound of the unfamiliar voice. She turned, saw a woman looming over her. The angle of the sun made it impossible to see the newcomer's features. Tituba started to stand.

The woman's arm came down in a sweeping arc. The object in her hand was heavy, and it connected solidly with the side of Tituba's head.

"Welcome to Deacon's Landing," the woman said.

Nothing but darkness after that.

A Real Pleasure

The first sensation of which Tituba became aware was the pounding in her head. It was this more than anything that forced her back to consciousness. She groaned, opened one eye. She could see nothing. All was black around her. She was inside, possibly below ground, judging by the dampness and chill of the air. She became aware her arms were raised above her head. She looked up at her hands, but she could not see the shackles around each wrist. It had been well over seventy years since she had felt cold steel on her wrists, and the memory was not a pleasant one. She tested them, found only a few inches of give. She groaned again.

She stood, planting her feet on what felt like dirt. It relieved the pain in her wrists if nothing else. She looked about, forcing her eyes to penetrate the total darkness around her. It was useless. This room could have been at the bottom of the ocean for all she could see. She closed her eyes and tilted her head back and concentrated on her breathing. That, at least, took her mind off the pounding in her head.

Her first instinct was to apparate to a safe place, perhaps the edge of town. She even started to summon her magick to do so. She stopped herself before the spell could be completed. Someone had gone to the trouble of bringing her here. Someone knew, or at least suspected, her true nature. Tituba decided to remain in place until she met this woman. If the situation deteriorated, she could always will herself away.

How long she stood there she could not say. At last, her attention was drawn by the sound of footsteps somewhere in the dark. A sliver of light appeared perhaps fifteen feet away. It elongated and expanded until Tituba could see an open door and the silhouette of a woman standing within its frame. The woman paused in the doorway. Although Tituba could not see her face, she knew the woman was examining her. Tituba remained silent, allowing her captor to make the first move.

Move she did. The woman reached for something on the other side of the door and produced a candelabra. Five candles it held, all alight, illuminating the space around Tituba.

Now that she could see, she found herself in a windowless room. The walls were stone of some kind, the floor dirt, as she had presumed. The exposed rafters on the ceiling were nearly ten feet above her head. More manacles were attached to the other walls, although she was the only current occupant of the room. The room was devoid of any furniture but a single chair in its center and the small yew table next to it.

The woman stepped across the threshold and closed the door behind her. She approached the chair and sat. The candelabra sat perched on the table. "I am going to ask questions. You will provide answers. That is the way of it."

Tituba said nothing. She searched the woman's eyes and found nothing but cruelty there. She pressed her lips together.

"Your name."

Tituba looked past the woman, her lips closed.

"You will tell me your name, or you will never leave this room alive. Name."

Tituba's gaze remained locked on a spot on the opposite wall. It was a small blemish, perhaps an old blood stain, but it was enough on which to fix her eyes.

"Very well," the woman said when it became apparent Tituba would remain silent. She leaned in a bit closer. "You sensed something in the statue, did you not? It's why you're here, you were drawn to it."

That caught Tituba's attention. Her eyes moved back to her woman jailer.

"I suspected as much," the woman continued. "I am here for the same reason. We should combine our efforts. Perhaps together we could locate this artifact and discover its nature."

You're lying, Tituba thought. *You might want to use me to get to this artifact but that is where our alliance will end. I'll wind up back in here, or worse.* What Tituba said was, "I am no fool." She smirked. She had indulged this woman long enough. Tituba apparated back to the statue . . .

But nothing happened. She remained in the room, arms raised above her head. She blinked, as if unwilling to believe the evidence of her own eyes. Never before had her magick failed her. She gathered her will and tried again.

"It won't work," the woman told her. "Whatever you're trying to do. We all seem to have one ability, do we not? That is what I have encountered over the decades. Each one of us can do one thing very well. Whatever your talent is, it will not function here. No magick works in my presence. That is *my* ability."

Tituba bore down and tried again. She received the same result. She exhaled slowly and closed her eyes. When she opened them again, she saw the woman had stood. She walked about the room slowly as if she were taking in a beautiful day in a park.

"It is unfortunate you chose to defy me. Together we may have done it. Your decision means simply I shall have to continue my efforts alone. So be it."

Tituba reached out to Neloye. She did not understand the link to her familiar, how it worked, exactly. If it was purely magickal then the leopard may be out of reach of her summons. Tituba thought the relationship between witch and familiar went deeper than simple magick. The two had bonded in a way Tituba had never thought to study. She and the big cat were a pair, plain and simple. That, at least, was how she had always looked at it. Now she hoped there was more to it than simple magick.

"My name is Tituba," she said.

The woman continued her slow walk about the room.

"I am from Barbados, though I have spent much of my time here in the colonies. I have encountered others like myself over the years, but none have had magick such as yours. And yes, I am here for whatever is hidden in that statue."

The woman stopped pacing and returned to the chair, although she did not sit. "I thought the loss of your magick might loosen your tongue. It is a pleasure to meet you, Tituba. My name is Anne. Anne Jacobs."

Tituba glanced up at the manacles holding her arms above her head. "A real pleasure."

"Oh, I will not be releasing you quite yet. We have a few matters which require discussion first. When I am satisfied with the information you provide, you will be free to go."

Do you really expect me to believe that? Not for nothing did you bring me down here. Come on, Neloye, where are you? This is no time to drag your paws upon the ground.

"What kind of information?"

"Where did you come from?" Anne asked. "You mentioned the colonies before. I require more specificity."

"You're an educated woman."

"As are you," Jacobs countered. She held up a hand. "Do not be concerned. I care not about the reading ability of a former slave. Yes, you were property once, I am certain. But no longer. I can see that in your eyes. Now, where are you from?"

"Mostly the Massachusetts Bay Colony, although I have visited Pennsylvania and New York. I have been as far south as Maryland, although only once." *Where are you, girl?*

"You should see Georgia," Anne told her. "It is quite beautiful, and far more temperate in clime."

"I'll add it to my list."

"The artifact that drew me to this godforsaken wilderness, the same which brought you here, what do you know of it?"

Tituba's eyes went to the door, waiting to see Neloye make her entrance. As of yet, Tituba did not know if the leopard had even heard her cry for help. If she hadn't . . .

Tituba returned her eyes to Anne Jacobs. "Nothing. I saw it in a dream, but it was vague, ill-defined. I do not know what it looks like, nor its purpose."

"I believe you," Anne replied. "For I have had the same dream." She approached Tituba until she stood no more than a foot from her. "I arrived here six months ago. As such, I have been allotted more time to investigate our mysterious artifact. Would it trouble you to know it no longer resides in the statue?"

Tituba started. "What?"

"Yes. Like you, I assumed it was either entombed within the stone or else buried beneath it. I believe it was, at one time, but it has since been moved. To where I cannot say yet."

Tituba shook her head. "No, that's impossible. I felt it a fortnight ago all the way in Springfield. It must be there."

"It is not. If it were, I would possess it already. And if I possessed it already, you and I would not be having this delightful conversation. You felt an echo of the artifact, as did I." She took a few steps away and resumed her place in the chair. "Doubtless you saw the man in the yellow robe. The thing in the sky, darker even than the night. Tell me, do you know the meaning behind these grave images?"

Tituba's head was spinning. How could the artifact not be hiding within or beneath the statue? She had felt the power herself. If Jacobs was telling the truth and what she had sensed was only the residual essence of the artifact, its power would be beyond anything Tituba had thus far encountered. Too, the woman knew of the man in the yellow robe and the creature in the sky. Tituba did not know their significance, but she knew they had some connection to this artifact.

Anne Jacobs reached into her sleeve and withdrew a dagger. Its handle was jeweled and quite beautiful. She twirled it slowly, allowed the iron of the blade to catch the light from the candles. "Iron. It is very old. It was gifted to me by King James himself. James I, I mean, not his fool of a great-grandson. Its blade has penetrated witch's flesh before." She ceased twirling the iron dagger and pointed it directly at Tituba. "It shall do so again if you do not tell me that which you know of the man-who-is-not-a-man in the yellow robe."

"You're a Pendle witch," Tituba said before she knew she would speak.

Anne Jacobs stopped in her tracks, and her eyes widened. Her surprise lasted only a moment. She wagged the dagger in Tituba's direction. "You *are* educated. My compliments. But you are incorrect. I am a Pendle witch no longer—I found it far more profitable to hunt them. I was His Majesty's witchfinder for a time. Hence, the iron dagger."

Tituba started. It took several moments to find her voice again. "You . . . *hunted* your own kind? Why?"

"Do not mistake our shared status for affection, Tituba. I care not for witches nor they for me. I care about Anne Jacobs and no other." She moved a few steps closer to Tituba. "Now tell me what I wish to know."

"You hunted your own kind," Tituba repeated, her voice a whisper. She stuttered before she could finally speak again. "You'll get nothing from me."

"Let us put that to the test, shall we?" Anne Jacobs covered the last few feet separating her from her captive. The iron blade pressed against Tituba's throat. "Tell me."

Tituba would have spat at her if her mouth and throat were not bone dry. She closed her eyes and waited for the dagger to be drawn across her throat. It turned out she needn't have worried. Neloye chose that moment to arrive.

An Empty Void

Tituba no longer felt the blade at her throat. She opened one eye, then the other, and she saw the big cat regarding her captor. The leopard moved into the room, shouldering the door open enough to allow her access. Her eyes scanned the room. She looked at Tituba chained to the wall before her eyes fell on Anne Jacobs.

The witchfinder turned, startled by the new arrival. Instinctively she brought the dagger up and pointed it at Neloye. "Back, beast!"

"I wouldn't point that at her," Tituba said. "Neloye has a tendency to dislike any who threaten her, or me."

"This, then, is your familiar?" Jacobs continued to point the blade at the leopard. She stepped around the small table, placing it between herself and the animal. "And you suspect it will save you? Have you forgotten my power? Your connection to it is severed. It no more obeys you than it would those foolish farmers outside."

Tituba froze. Was Jacobs right? She reached within herself, felt for the familiar presence of the leopard . . . and found nothing. Where she had felt Neloye for so many decades, there was nothing but an empty void. The leopard was no longer connected to her in any way. It had to have happened when Neloye entered the room. Jacobs's power had removed the familiar's link to Tituba. That meant Tituba had rung the dinner bell . . . and she was shackled to the wall.

Neloye had locked her eyes on Anne Jacobs. The hair on her back stood straight up, her lips pulled back and revealed her fangs. Saliva dripped onto the dirt. The leopard growled.

Jacobs raised her dagger, ready to strike.

Neloye leaped the ten feet which separated the two. She crashed into Jacobs, and they both wound up on the floor in a heap of thrashing muscle. Teeth and iron flared and tore at flesh and cloth. The air was filled with snarling and screaming.

Tituba could not make out much of what was happening. The table had overturned, and the candelabra went flying. Three of the five candles had been extinguished. The two remaining candles succeeded only in throwing shadows around the room.

"Neloye! I need your help, girl! We have to get away from her!" All Tituba needed was to be free of the shackles. Once outside the room, she could place herself and Neloye fifty miles away from Anne Jacobs and her iron dagger.

The candles stabilized enough that Tituba could now see Neloye had the upper hand. She was atop Anne Jacobs, one of the witchfinder's arms locked in the leopard's jaws. Her other arm, however, was the one that wielded the dagger. Amid the screaming and growling, she brought the blade down, and it pierced the animal's shoulder. Neloye released her grip on Jacobs's arm and backed away.

Jacobs rose to her knees. Blood dripped from her wounded arm and her cheeks where the animal's claws had raked her face. She leveled the dagger again, but her hand shook. "Away! Get away!"

Neloye circled the room, her eyes locked on Jacobs. She paid no heed to the bound woman. Anne Jacobs circled the room as well, keeping the chair and the remains of the table between her and the leopard. When the door was at her back, she moved toward it.

"As the beast tears your flesh, try to remember it was I who sent you to Lucifer," she told Tituba. She backed toward the door.

Neloye leaped again. This time the leopard aimed for the hand holding the dagger. She succeeded in clamping down on Jacobs's wrist. The wounded witchfinder screamed and dropped the dagger. Neloye thrashed left and then right, jerking Anne Jacobs off her feet. The witchfinder recovered and kicked at Neloye with both feet. She connected with the animal's jaw, and Neloye backed away, growling.

Jacobs was on her feet and through the door before Neloye could recover. The door slammed closed behind her. Tituba heard a key in the lock and then Anne Jacobs was gone.

"Good girl, Neloye, good girl."

Neloye turned to her. The leopard's eyes held no hint of recognition. Her lips pulled back from her teeth. She approached slowly, her fur sticky with her own blood as well as Jacobs's. She growled.

"Neloye?" The leopard's stance, the way she moved, Tituba had seen it many times before. She was ready to attack. Tituba pondered what it would feel like when Neloye's fangs pierced her flesh.

The leopard pounced.

Her giant paws landed on Tituba's shoulders. Instead of sharp fangs ripping pieces of her flesh, she instead felt a wet tongue on her cheeks. Tituba opened one eye and saw her familiar again.

At the same moment, she felt the magick return to her. In an instant, she apparated herself and the leopard to a spot outside Deacon's Landing, deep in the woods where none would see them.

No Dreams

That night, Tituba built a fire, and Neloye provided a few squirrels for dinner. They sat beside each other and felt the warmth of the flames. The new bandage around Neloye's shoulder retained its original color, which meant the bleeding had stopped and the healing was well under way. Tituba was grateful for her knowledge of the healing properties of some plants. As the leopard lay down to rest, her head placed comfortably in Tituba's lap, the witch thought back to the windowless room and Anne Jacobs.

Her magick, the ability to nullify the magick of others, had gone with her when she fled the room. Was that the deciding factor? Had she remained on the other side of that door, would the link with Neloye not have reestablished itself in time? Was the link ever truly broken to begin with? Had Tituba's fate rested in the hands of Anne Jacobs and her decision to flee instead of staying just out of reach of Neloye? Was fate truly that random? Well, yes, it was. But Tituba felt there was more to it.

Perhaps she had never been in any real danger from her familiar. Perhaps the big cat was simply reacting to the situation, to having been stabbed, to having been in a battle with a hostile witch.

Or perhaps she truly would have attacked Tituba. Neither of them would ever likely know the answer to that question. Tituba stroked the leopard's fur and listened to the slight snore she produced in response.

That night, she did not dream of the artifact, nor of the man-who-is-not-a-man in the yellow robe, nor of the giant beast in the sky. She did not dream at all, in fact. When she awoke in the morning, Neloye was sitting next to her, looking at her and waiting for them to begin their day.

Tituba still knew nothing of the artifact, including its location. Its power must be far beyond anything she had encountered before if its echo was enough to be felt the fifty or so miles between them. It would require more study, that much was certain. But that was for another day. One day, Tituba would locate the artifact, and if she had to deal with Anne Jacobs in the process, then so be it.

She patted her familiar's head. Neloye purred her approval.

Jenn: Part V

Jenn was dreaming. She sat perched atop the peak of her roof, the moon shining high above her head. Stars twinkled in the night sky. A soft summer breeze tousled her hair as she looked out over the sleeping neighborhood. During tonight's flight over the town, she'd thought about the last couple of days. She'd spoken with several fellow witches and had heard a number of fascinating tales featuring a variety of different familiars. What she'd discovered boiled down to three things: 1) a familiar could be a mutually beneficial and trusted companion; 2) if and when the time came to choose one, she would feel it in her head and in her heart; and 3) taking on a familiar was a life-altering experience. For the moment, at least, the only thing of which Jenn was certain was that she was not ready for such a commitment.

Earlier in the day, when she'd gotten home, she'd wandered the yard looking for the white owl. It was nowhere to be found. She studied the branches of the large tree outside her bedroom window, and even now, in her dream, she saw no sign of the owl perched anywhere within its branches. Her only contact with the bird had been in sleep, and as far as she knew, the real, actual owl had moved on some time ago. Had she let her dreams and imagination get the best of her? The more she considered it, the more she believed that to be the case.

Jenn soon heard a rustling sound she recognized to be the flapping of wings. Bubonivis, the white owl of her dreams, landed with a plop beside her on the ridge of the roof.

"Well, hello, my dear friend," hooted the owl. It stumbled over its own claws and nearly tumbled down the slope of the roof. In a flurry of flapping wings, it righted itself, swiveling its head in Jenn's direction, its orange eyes reflecting the moonlight.

"Er—hi, Bob," replied Jenn. "Where have you been? I've been looking for you."

"You have?" the owl hooted. Jenn could sense joy in his tone. He hopped around excitedly on the peak of the roof. "Okay, I'll tell you. It was going to be a surprise, but I've been busy searching . . ."

"Searching?" echoed Jenn.

"Yes, I've been searching . . . for a present—for my new best friend. A present for you!"

Oh great, she thought. "Your last gift was more than generous." Her stomach twisted at the thought of the tiny animal corpses she'd found littering her front steps. "You really don't need to do that," she said. "I'm sure you have, uh, more important things to do."

Bubonivis appeared to think for a moment. "No, not really." The owl's head swiveled first in one direction and then the other before he continued. "I spent the whole day looking for it. I was about to give up—but then I found it!"

Jenn wasn't sure what to so say. The owl seemed dedicated to pleasing her, albeit in a very misguided way.

"You just stay right here," said Bubonivis, "and I'll fetch it!" Before Jenn could respond, the owl flew down the back side of the roof and vanished from view. Although a bit peculiar, Bubonivis seemed thoughtful and considerate, a trait missing from many human beings these days. And so, Jenn steeled herself to happily accept whatever disgusting tidbit the owl intended to gift to her.

When Bubonivis returned several moments later, Jenn was surprised to see not a dead carcass in the owl's beak but a crumpled piece of paper. Bubonivis landed beside her and thrust the weather-worn page into her hand.

"What do we have here?" she asked, glancing in the owl's direction. Carefully she stretched the paper flat against her leg and smoothed out the worst of the wrinkles. She struggled to make out the letters and symbols in the moonlight—but gradually, the inks came into focus. She inhaled sharply as recognition kicked in. It was one of the irreplaceable missing pages of the ancient grimoire that she and Aunt Celia were working to restore! And somehow, against all odds, Bubonivis had located it. For her.

Jenn felt her eyes begin to water as she gauged the magnitude of thoughtfulness and effort that had gone into the gesture. The old spell book had been one of her deceased grandmother's most significant possessions. "But how did you know?" she asked, turning to the owl.

"My dear friend is pleased?" Bubonivis hooted. When Jenn nodded, the owl jumped into the air in an excited flutter of wings. Settling back onto its perch, the owl explained, "I've been watching you for several days. I was there, outside, when you and the other witch sorted the pages. That was when I learned that you sought them. The perfect gift, no?"

"The perfect gift," responded Jenn with a smile, ignoring for the moment that the bird had been stalking her. "I can't wait to tell Aunt Celia. She'll be very pleased. I—"

And that was when Jenn remembered that the missing page, her nightly flights, Bubonivis—all of them—were just part of her elaborate recurring dream. She was suddenly hit with a wave of melancholy.

With the wrinkled paper in hand, she gestured toward the world around them. "I—I'm just sad," she continued, "that none of this is real." When she looked back at Bubonivis, she sensed dismay in his feathery features.

"But I don't understand," Bubonivis hooted. "Why would you say such a thing?"

"Because it's all just a dream," she said with a disappointed shake of the head. "Not that it matters, but please tell me—why me? Why the interest in me?"

The happy enthusiasm that had filled Bubonivis was gone, and Jenn knew that she was the one who had killed it. That knowledge only deepened her own sadness.

"The moment I saw you," the owl replied somberly, "I just knew you were special."

A tear flowed down Jenn's cheek. The owl's words had touched her. "And you would like to be my familiar?" she asked, already knowing the answer.

"I'd be most honored," said Bubonivis. "If my dear friend would have me as such." For just a moment, the owl's cheerfulness returned.

"Well," she said, confusion and frustration sharpening her tongue, "you should know then that I am in no way ready for such an arrangement." She felt bad the moment the words left her lips, but it was too late to take them back. Bubonivis, with a look of devastation, turned, took to the air, and soared off into the darkness.

Jenn took a deep breath, releasing it through her mouth. *What have I done?* She glanced at the crumpled piece of paper in her hand, a thoughtful gift from a thoughtful admirer. A gift that she no longer felt she deserved. As if in punishment, a gust of wind tore the grimoire page from her fingers. She watched it shoot skyward before fluttering off into the night.

Jenn sat in silence on the peak of the roof and cried.

The following morning, Jenn woke to sunlight streaming through her window's open curtains. Tossing aside the sheet, she swung her legs over the bed and rubbed her eyes.

Last night's dream still haunted her—her unkind words to Bubonivis, the owl's belief that he, the dream, and the ancient grimoire page were all real. She knew they were just figments of her imagination, of course. She couldn't talk to owls, much less fly through the night sky! Why then did the encounter trouble her so?

She stood, stepped into her slippers, and crossed to the window. Fighting common sense, she peered through the glass, her eyes traveling up and down the giant tree outside her window, hoping to see some trace of the owl—of Bubonivis, the white owl of her dreams. She searched branch after branch but, as expected, none of them contained the peculiar, adorable, adoring bird.

Jenn decided it was time to move on with her day. She quickly hopped in the shower, brushed her teeth, and then dried her hair. When she was finished, she pulled on some jeans and a fresh top from her dresser. She had no firm plans for the day, but she knew she had to do something to shake herself out of the funk she'd woken up in. Jenn decided the best thing to do was get out of the house.

She grabbed her shoes and phone and started for the bedroom door, but something stopped her. She glanced at the window and decided to take one final look. Again, she approached the window and peered through the glass. She scanned the tree once more, but there were no obvious signs of the white owl.

You're being silly, she thought. *What were you expecting to find? You're losing it, Jenn, old girl.*

Jenn sighed, ready to give up—but then she spotted something high up in the canopy. It was far too small to be Bubonivis, but it was also too light in color to be a part of the tree . . .

She took out her phone, pulled up the camera, and zoomed in on the object. It was still too far to make out. She snapped a photo and then opened it, zooming in further with two fingers.

She studied the image, disappointed to find what appeared to be trash—just a discarded sheet of paper, weathered and worn, snagged on a limb . . .

Or was it?

Jenn gasped. Her heart began to beat faster. *Could it be?* Against all odds and her own common sense, Jenn believed it to be true:

She'd just found Bubonivis's gift. It was the missing grimoire page.

It had been ages since Jenn had last climbed a tree—not since elementary school, with Zach—and she was way out of practice. She stepped off the topmost rung of her father's ladder and pulled herself up onto the nearest branch. Carefully, she stood, reaching about for handholds as she stared up through the boughs.

The tree towered over her, and she still had so far to go. If the missing grimoire page was up there, it was somewhere high above her, way out of sight. For a moment, she considered turning back. The climb would be dangerous, but she had to know for certain: Was the lost sheet real? Was any of it real? Her dreams? Bubonivis?

Onward and upward—that was her path. The answers lay ahead.

As Jenn climbed, she considered the implications of finding the grimoire page. If it turned out to be real, then it would follow that everything else was as well. The odds against the loose sheet ending up stuck in her tree the very night after she dreamed about it were astronomical. Could it be that she had been sleepwalking? Sleep *flying*? The idea sounded like nonsense. And what of Bubonivis? Part of her wanted him to be real, so that she could apologize, make amends. The other part of her was terrified and not ready to accept that she'd met a potential familiar, a creature that had been kind to her, a being that could forever alter her life. What Jenn had told Bubonivis was true—she was not ready for such a commitment.

As Jenn passed the thirty-foot mark, she paused to catch her breath. Looking out over her yard, she saw that she was above the roofline of her house. Out front, Mrs. Jankowski from up the street was being yanked down the sidewalk by her cocker spaniel, Hercules, who seemed eager to sniff everything in his path. Mr. Smith, her next-door neighbor, was vacuuming his swimming pool in preparation for his granddaughters' daily summer visit. It was a typical morning in Windsor, and yet here Jenn was, climbing a fifty-foot tree in her side-yard.

If only I really could fly, she thought, smiling to herself, *this would be a whole lot easier.*

At the forty-foot mark, Jenn spotted the weathered piece of paper, wedged in a clump of leaves, about fifteen feet up and to her left. To reach it she'd have to make her way along a thick bough that stretched a dozen feet from the trunk. It would be, by far, the most perilous and risky part of the climb. Carefully, she stepped out onto the thick branch.

She looked down at the lawn far below. Fortunately, she'd never been particularly afraid of heights. One thing was certain, however: a fall from this height would break bones—and very likely, far worse.

She followed the bough for several feet until the branch she was holding onto for balance shifted beyond her reach. She'd come too far to turn back now, and for the first time she wondered if she'd be able to climb back down. She reached for her pocket, only then remembering that she'd left her phone at the base of the ladder. She was worried she'd drop it. In retrospect, the decision had been shortsighted. But then again, if she got stuck, she could always shout for help.

Jenn studied the bough in front of her. To cross it on foot would be like walking a tightrope without a net. She'd have to sit, straddle it, and slide forward inch by treacherous inch. She bent her knees and lowered herself slowly, her hands stretched out before her. When she could sink no further, she let herself drop onto her rear end. Falling forward, she hugged the branch with both arms to stabilize her hold.

Wow, that was scarier than I expected, she thought as she rose to a seated position. Jenn shifted her butt slowly forward, keeping her eyes on the prize. The crumpled piece of paper was now a mere five or six feet away. It hung wedged in a cluster of leaves on an overhanging branch.

The bough grew steadily narrower the farther she traveled, and soon it began to dip slightly under her weight. Smaller leaf-covered branches began to sprout from the bough, making passage more difficult. At last, however, the weathered page was in reach. Jenn let go of the rough, bark-covered surface and lurched upward, her hand closing about the old sheet of paper.

Success!

Jenn straightened the page, revealing the inked Latin script and the archaic symbols that she'd last seen the night before. There was no doubt left. It was real, and therefore, so was Bubonivis. Her heart beat excitedly out of her chest.

Thrill turned to terror as a loud wooden *crack* issued from somewhere behind her. The bough on which she sat dropped suddenly, pitching Jenn forward and tossing her free of the tree. Jenn suddenly felt weightless. Panic filled her as she realized she was, more likely than not, about to die.

She tumbled downward five feet, and then ten. Her life passed before her as time slowed to a crawl. She thought of her family. She thought of Zach and their friendship, a relationship that could have become so much more had she let it. She thought of Nate and Marc and how her life had changed so much for the better since they'd arrived in town. She thought of Aunt Celia and Tee and of the revelation that she, too, was a witch. She thought of Malleus Hodge's banishment and of her friend Douglas who had also died on that fateful night. She thought of Courtney, Alex, and Neloye, and of Blaze and Corvin, all of whom had made unique impressions on her life. She thought of Bubonivis, the peculiar great horned owl and potential familiar with whom she'd made a connection and with whom she'd never be able to make amends . . .

Despair filled Jenn as the ground rushed up to greet her. She barely registered the feathery white shape speeding toward her at lightning speed. Bubonivis reached Jenn mere seconds before impact.

Bubonivis?

The owl soared beneath her, placing his body between Jenn and the ground, as if, somehow, he could soften the impact with his feathered, soon-to-be flattened corpse.

You poor, dear, sweet bird.

And that was when something truly amazing happened.

Upon contact with the owl, a flood of feelings rushed through her. She felt Bubonivis's unconditional acceptance of her, his desire to please her, and his need to be needed. She felt his awkwardness, his fears and insecurities—characteristics that she too had dealt with in the past.

And these feelings awoke compatible emotions within herself: Jenn's need to be accepted and appreciated, to care and nurture others, to be the best person she knew how to be.

I'm sorry, Jenn communicated nonverbally, somehow knowing that Bubonivis would hear her.

Thank you, dear friend, responded the owl. *I forgive you, of course.*

And in that moment, Jenn knew exactly what she needed to do. She felt it in her head, heart, and soul. *Will you be my familiar?* As soon as she formed the words in her mind, she was flooded with joy—Bubonivis's and her own.

Yes, yes, and yes, my dear friend!

Thank you, my dear Bubonivis!

Their interaction had lasted only an instant, but Jenn was quickly running out of time. With a new sense of hope and purpose, she knew she had to act quickly. She had to try to save both Bubonivis and herself. She reached for the owl, taking the bird into her arms, and then, with every ounce of concentration, self-control, and self-discipline at her disposal, she willed herself to stop falling. She willed herself to fly.

And somehow, boosted by her familiar's own flying skill, adoration, and confidence in her—it worked.

Jenn hurried up the grand staircase to the second floor of the Watson mansion, on her way to the artifact room. She'd called Aunt Celia earlier with the news that she'd acquired a familiar and was looking forward to introducing Bubonivis to her friends. Aunt Celia promised to call everyone together as soon as possible.

She stepped into the hallway, pausing to massage her sore behind. Her earlier attempt at flight had been only moderately successful, but it *had* saved her life. She found it incredible to think that she'd flown with such ease on those nights when she'd thought she was dreaming. Fully awake and in full daylight, the experience had been something quite different. A crash landing and a bruised bottom had shown her that she still had a lot to learn about takeoffs and landings. In fact, without Bubonivis, she wasn't sure she could have even done as well as she had.

Jenn's near-death experience and her adoption of a familiar had left her in exceptional spirits. She was high on life and ready to embrace her future, wherever it led. And that would require making some adjustments, the first of which involved her relationship with Zach. Up until now she'd preferred the comfort of the status quo over the uncertainty of change—but no more. She intended to live life to its fullest.

Up ahead, she could hear the happy chatter of her friends. She recognized the voices of Nate and Alex and Zach, and when she walked into the room, she saw that others had gathered as well. Aunt Celia and Tee were there, seated at the table. Marc sat with them, Blaze squirming on his lap. Corvin was perched in his cage along one wall, Neloye lay sprawled out on the hearth before the fireplace.

"Hi, Jenn," said Aunt Celia, standing to greet her.

Jenn smiled, wrapping her arms around the older woman and squeezing her tightly.

"Oh my," said Aunt Celia with a grin.

When Jenn stepped back, she pressed the rumpled grimoire sheet that she'd been carrying into Aunt Celia's hand. "We can bind the pages into the book this afternoon," said Jenn enthusiastically. Aunt Celia nodded.

Jenn then made her rounds, giving each person present a firm hug. When she got to Zach, she placed her hands on either side of his head and pulled him in for a kiss. He stepped back with a surprised yet pleased expression on his face.

"What was that for?" he whispered.

"I've been doing a lot of thinking," she replied. "Can we talk later?"

"You got it," he said with a smile that matched her own.

"So, what's the big news?" asked Nate. He smirked, waving a finger toward Zach. "Did it have something to do with that?"

"No," said Jenn. "Actually, it's something else." Her eyes scanned the group, noting the curiosity and excitement on each person's face as they waited for her to continue. "Let me first say thank you, so much, for coming. You all mean so much to me. The past several weeks have been life altering for all of us. Not the least of which, for me, has been the fact that I inherited ancestral magick that I never knew existed." Jenn glanced around the room to find everyone listening intently. Marc nodded in response, as did Tee and Alex. "Over the last few days, each of you has been instrumental in my coming to terms with the fact that today I'm a different person. We've all experienced hardships. We've all been afraid. But together, we've gotten through all of it. And so, I wanted you to know that this morning, I made a life-altering decision." She paused for dramatic effect. "I've taken on a familiar of my very own!"

"Wow, really?" Alex was the first to respond.

Jenn nodded as her friends traded surprised looks.

"I didn't know you were looking for one," said Nate, "but if you're happy, we're happy. Congratulations!"

Everyone else tossed out words of agreement and encouragement.

"Hey, where is it?" asked Marc, looking around the room.

"Please tell me it's a winged monkey!" added Zach. "I've always wanted a winged monkey!"

Jenn laughed. "He's nearby. Let me introduce you. His name is Bob."

"Your familiar's name is Bob?" said Tee, who had remained silent until that moment. Her nose wrinkled as if she'd smelled something horrible. Her expression changed to one of embarrassment when she realized that everyone was looking at her. "Oh, dear. I mean, that doesn't sound like a proper name for—" She placed her hand over her mouth, cutting herself off. This set off a round of laughter.

"It's actually Bubonivis, Bob for short," said Jenn with a grin. She stepped over to the window and opened it wide. *Bubonivis, come meet my friends,* she called out to the owl without speaking.

Several seconds later, she heard a familiar flapping of wings. "Here he is, everyone. Please welcome—"

A feathery white shape came into view. It flew straight for the nearest window. Unfortunately, it wasn't the window that Jenn had just opened. With a loud thud, Bubonivis bounced off the glass and dropped like a brick.

Jenn and several others gasped. *Are you okay?* she called with her mind. Jenn leaned out the window to see where he had fallen. The owl was already circling around for another attempt.

Yes, I'm fine, he replied. *Sorry, dear friend.* Bubonivis landed on the sill a moment later, his claws tightly grasping the woodwork. Jenn was relieved that the owl was okay.

You still fly better than I do, she said. She hadn't mentioned her unreliable new ability to anyone. Out loud she said: "Here he is, everyone! Say hello to Bubonivis!"

Jenn smiled as Zach, Nate, and Alex joined her at the window. Marc, Aunt Celia, and Tee joined them a moment later.

"He's no winged monkey," said Zach, "but I think he's cool!"

"Me too, I love owls," added Marc, stroking the top of Bubonivis's head.

The others took turns welcoming Bubonivis into their unconventional little family.

You're going to fit right in, thought Jenn, feeling happy and hopeful.

"Hoo-h'hoo-hoo-hoo!" responded the owl.

Sometime later . . .

The old woman glided down the dark, dank, cobweb-filled corridor, her feet floating several inches above the floor. Her long skirts, remnants of an earlier era, trailed behind her, yet they left no evidence of her passage in the thick dust. She made no effort to avoid the cobwebs. She didn't need to. She passed right through them.

When she reached the wall-sized mirror at the end of the passageway, she paused to examine her reflection. Her once-dark hair was now a white-gray, tied in a bun behind her head. Her eyes were sunken and dark. Lines marred her once-smooth skin. She'd been eighty-eight when she died, and so she would remain, her ghostly appearance a hideous reminder of her final days of life.

Oh, how simply dreadful, she thought. She shrugged. *Nothing to be done about it now.*

Tentatively she reached for the glass, but unlike last time, her hand met resistance. She could no longer pass through—someone on the other side had barred her passage out of the mirror realm. It told her everything she needed to know. Well, nearly everything. They'd found and triggered the miniature mansion, the trap she'd left behind—but had they escaped it? She'd be pleased if they hadn't—but it would be far more beneficial to her if they had . . .

She stepped back and spoke the words to a spell. On the floor in front of her appeared a pile of dolls, translucent and ghostlike. There were five of them, the nooses still wrapped about their throats.

She cackled with glee as she stooped to collect them.

About the Authors

RANDE GOODWIN is a full-time IT professional and part-time raptor trainer (the prehistoric kind). In his free time, he enjoys reading and travel, restoring vintage Borg drones, dusting vamps in Sunnydale, and being one with the Force. Oh, and writing is fun too. He lives in New England with his wife, two daughters, and three dogs. See what he's up to at: www.randegoodwin.com

JOSEPH J. CHRISTIANO has been an avid reader since he could hold a book in his hands. On the rare occasions he's not writing or reading, he spends his time watching his beloved New York Yankees, driving his 1968 GTO and spending time with his family and his dogs. He lives in Connecticut's Naugatuck Valley. For further frightening stories in the fictional town of Deacon's Landing, Connecticut, check out the following novels by Joe:

Dark Annie
Old Ghosts
The Lords of Greystone

The Witches of Windsor: Book 1

The Witchfinder's Serpent

A NOVEL

RANDE GOODWIN

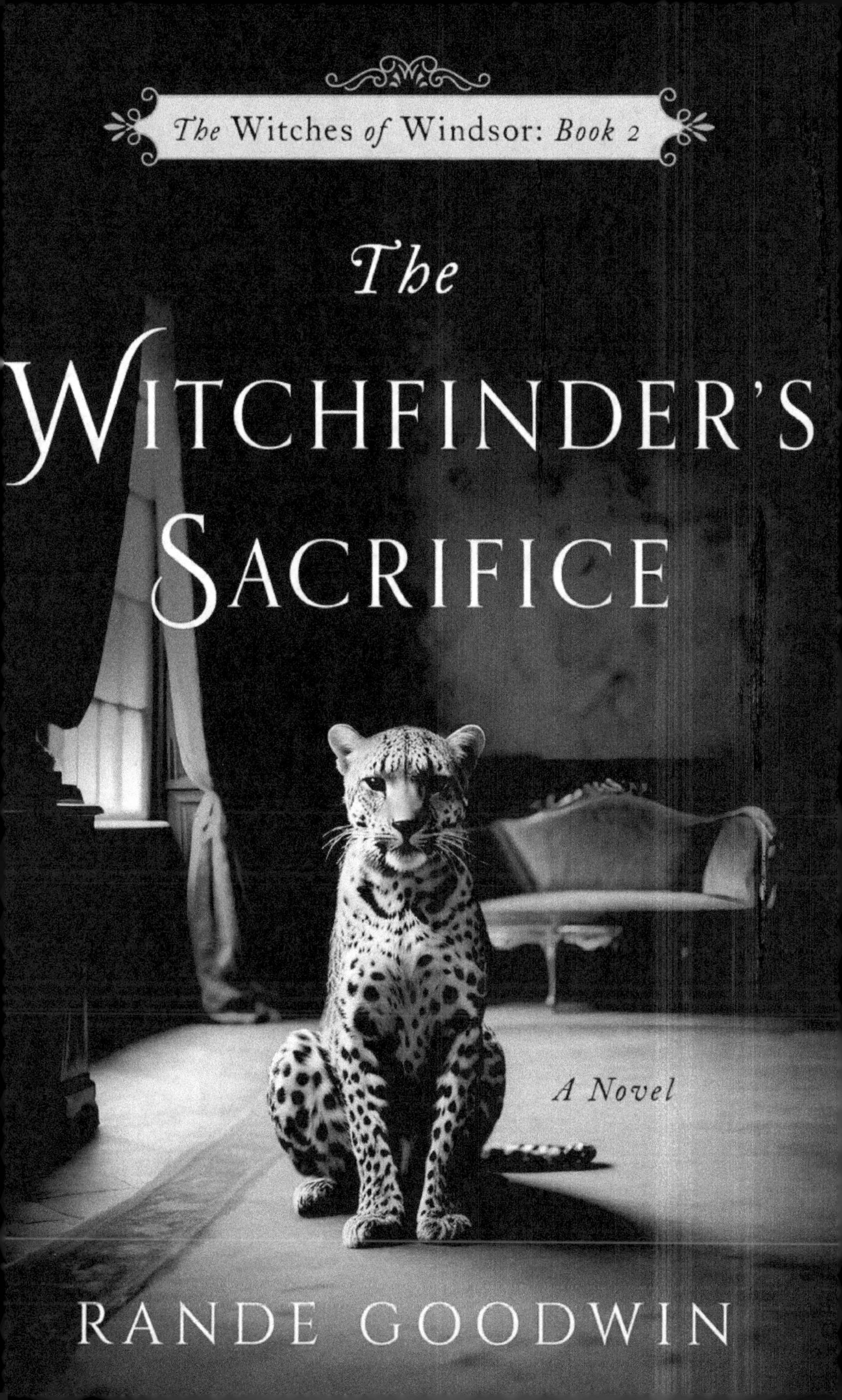

The Witches *of* Windsor: *Book 2*

The Witchfinder's Sacrifice

A Novel

RANDE GOODWIN

The Witches *of* Windsor

The Witchfinder's Familiar

An Anthology

Rande Goodwin

www.ingramcontent.com/pod-product-compliance
Lightning Source LLC
Chambersburg PA
CBHW060545310726
48982CB00009B/1384/J

* 9 7 9 8 9 9 2 5 5 3 6 0 4 *